A DEADLY SNARE

Sara Mitchell

ACCENT BOOKS
Denver, Colorado

ACCENT BOOKS
A division of Accent Publications, Inc.
12100 West Sixth Avenue
P.O. Box 15337
Denver, Colorado 80215

Library of Congress Catalog Card Number 89-81809

ISBN 0-89636-263-9

For "Sara I":
an advisor and loving critic
an encourager and faithful fan
an inspiration—and—
my mother

ACKNOWLEDGMENTS

Thanks to Ed Kirtley, Public Education Specialist, Colorado Springs Fire Department.

Thanks, as well, to my wonderful, long-suffering husband Phil, who provided a wealth of significant details to insure accuracy.

"A fortune made by a lying tongue is a fleet-ing vapor and a deadly snare." (Proverbs 21:6, NIV)

PROLOGUE

London, England, 1944

The heavy door closed behind him, snuffing out all sounds of the party. Fog—wet, cold, almost impenetrable—enclosed him before he took two steps; he paused to tug the collar of his coat over his uniform, shivering in the dank November night. The silence rang in his ears.

Mindful of the nature of his errand, he quickened his steps, hurrying down the rough, largely ruined walk. The last V-2, General Avery had told him while they pretended to chat, had hit only two blocks away the previous night.

He stopped suddenly, skin prickling. Off to his left ran the Thames, where the mournful wail of a passing trawler rang with a muffled echo, then died in the dripping fog. He lifted his hand, surreptitiously patting his left chest to make sure the information was still securely in place.

There is was again—the scrape of a shoe on stone. He melted with eerie silence into the shadow of a brick wall and waited.

Droplets of fog condensed in his hair, on his face, dampening his neck even with the protection of his heavy coat. His mouth flattened into a grim line of ruthless determination. He knew they'd sent someone after him—he'd been followed from France but thought he'd lost them when he hit London. They were worse than bloodhounds, more lethal than the deadly rockets. And they wouldn't quit because what he had discovered was too important.

7

He clenched his teeth and waited.

Just a couple more hours—that's all I need. . . .*General Avery had promised him Christmas leave after he passed the diary on. After fourteen months of unending nightmare, he could catch a hop to the States, and give Molly and the kids a present they'd prayed about for three years now.*

Slowly, eyes and ears tuned to even a change in the wind, he resumed his stealthy path to the car.

It's almost over, *he thought, though there was little satisfaction. The damage nine supposedly loyal Americans had dealt their country was incalculable.* They oughta line 'em up in the path of one of those V-2's. . .or send 'em to one of Hitler's death camps.

He fought the rage at their treason, knowing anger could blind him as completely as the unrelenting London fog.

Does Jesus mind if we're angry at the Nazis, Daddy?"

Justeen, so solemn and serious, her four-year-old face lifted to him as she asked the question. . .he could barely remember what she looked like now. It had been so long. Too long. But he'd be home for Christmas.

Even if he'd never get any medals, even if General Avery had warned him the whole affair would be buried in the bowels of the War Department, he knew he'd done what he had to do—would do again if it meant exposing traitors.

There was the car. It loomed just ahead, a dark, shapeless mass. His fingers burrowed inside his coat pocket, closing over the key. He slid in, breathing a sigh of relief as he closed the door with a barely audible snick. Almost home free. *The hour or so drive wouldn't be much fun, but he'd done it. He'd done it!*

I'm coming home, darlin'. It's been too long, but I'm—

The back of his neck prickled in warning. He ducked and turned automatically, but it was too late.

A muffled thunk was the only sound the silencer allowed to escape from the pistol as it was fired at point blank range.

8

CHAPTER 1

Washington, D.C., August—present day

She was late.

Paige glanced at her watch, crammed the last bite of a granola bar in her mouth, grimaced, and took another minute to drink some juice. Mom would have blistered her ears—but then Mom wasn't pulling double duty as a research assistant for two demanding men.

Actually, Paige decided with reluctant fairness a few minutes later as she fought beltway morning rush hour traffic, Jonah couldn't be described as "demanding." In the six months she'd been helping him research his next book, he hadn't even raised his voice.

...And he had a very nice voice. Paige lifted a hand to make sure her hair was in place, then caught herself. Making a face at the rearview mirror, she wriggled her shoulders, then her neck, to ease some of the tension.

It was going on seven, with an anemic sun sluggishly shining through a fast evaporating mist. But at least the morning light softened a little the crush of exhaust-belching vehicles creeping along like a slow moving convoy of multi-colored ants.

I should have brought him coffee and doughnuts. I doubt if there's anything in the house worth eating besides those wretched jars of peanuts Professor K. stashes in every room.

Her hands tightened on the wheel. She had to stop thinking like that. If Jonah was hungry, he could get himself something to eat. He was not—repeat, *not*—her responsibility.

She finally made it to the professor's house, parking in the driveway. Eight-seventeen. She hated being late.

Forcing her thoughts aside, she turned the engine off, realizing Jonah was late, too. His Harley was nowhere in sight.

"Exasperating man," Paige muttered, though her gaze was indulgent as she surveyed the jungle of Professor Kittridge's yard. Her eccentric boss refused to consider a townhome or apartment, obstinately clinging to the house he and his now dead wife had lived in for thirty years.

Paige forced herself to move with her usual calm, unhurried efficiency, unwilling to arrive flushed and rattled on the doorstep even when she was the only one here. She paused to sniff a late summer rose, speculating at what her mother could do in this wildly overgrown yard.

Her ear caught a faint sound.

Frowning, Paige straightened and peered toward the picture window, barely visible through the tangled branches of some crepe myrtle. Professor K. wasn't supposed to be here—he always left for his office on the campus at Georgetown by six o'clock to avoid the traffic and crush of commuters taking the Metro.

Puzzled and a little concerned, Paige climbed the steps, pressed the buzzer a couple of times, then opened the door with her key.

She paused just inside the threshold, the hairs on the back of her neck suddenly lifting with an uneasy sensation that something was wrong. "Professor?" she called out in the silence of the dark, musty-smelling entrance hall.

The fedora and cane were gone from the bentwood coat-rack—Professor Kittridge was definitely not at home. Paige

10

walked slowly down the hall to the bedroom he had turned into his "World War II" room.

There it was again—a soft sort of shuffling, like shoes muffled by carpet or clothing brushing against a wall. It had come from down the hall, toward the living room. Her mouth suddenly dry, her heartbeat accelerating, Paige gingerly pushed open the half-closed door to the World War II room. It was empty, but—

"No! Oh, no!" Her stunned eyes moved over the room, absorbing a sight far more devastating to a dedicated historian than the presence of a mere burglar.

The room had been torn apart with methodical savagery. Books lay in scattered piles all over the floor—the floor-to-ceiling shelves that covered two walls were stripped bare, facing her with macabre nakedness. Papers had been flung helter-skelter and littered every surface in the room. The files of the antique oak cabinet gaped open, its contents disgorged and flung about in mountainous disarray.

"What's going on here? What happened?"

Paige gasped, a choked-off scream caught in her throat as she whipped about so abruptly her shoe slipped on the cover of a book. Hard arms closed around her. She struggled, shoving against a hard chest. "Let go—let me—" She suddenly wilted, collapsing against the man who obligingly hugged her, then gently lifted her away a little.

"Paige?" Jonah's indigo-ink blue eyes scanned her face, then lifted to survey the ransacked room. Just for a moment, his hands tightened reassuringly on her upper arms. His strength and warmth flooded her with a bewildering sense of safety.

Rattled by the shock of her discovery, Jonah's sudden appearance, and her own confusing response, Paige blurted out, "I couldn't help it. It was like this when I got here. I'm sorry, Jonah. I'm—" She clamped her jaw shut, then carefully eased herself free from his arms. Rubbing her elbows with her hands, she stared into those mesmerizing eyes and tried to compose herself. "I haven't checked the rest of the house—the living room wasn't touched. But I—"

His hand covered her mouth. "Shh—I heard a noise."

Paige nodded vigorously, her eyes stretched wide. Jonah smiled down at her, deepening the creases in his cheeks on either side of a bushy auburn moustache. The broad hand covering her mouth lifted, brushed her cheek.

"Stay here—don't move," he whispered, then melted out into the hall with a soundlessness more frightening than his abrupt appearance.

Paige crept to the door, trying to control her tattered breathing and the tremors attacking her limbs. She watched Jonah move down the hall like a panther poised for the kill, his body alert, latent with streamlined power.

If she hadn't worked for the last six months with a laid-back, self-effacing man who constantly misplaced his glasses, then grinned like a sheepish boy when Paige pointed them out, she would have run screaming for the nearest window.

This man looked—dangerous. The burnt mahogany hair was still tousled from his motorcycle helmet; muscles Paige had never noticed rippled across his shoulders and back through the thin knit weave of his shirt. He stopped, crouched in a position to attack.

From the far end of the house came the grating sound of an unwilling window being opened. In a flash, Jonah sprinted down the hall and disappeared. Paige followed more slowly, her body rigid with shock, fear—and amazement.

Noise exploded from the other side of the kitchen, and seconds later a dark clad, stocking-faced man charged into the living room, Jonah close behind. The intruder turned and lashed out with a poker grabbed from the fireplace. Jonah ducked, feinted to the right, then in a series of lightning moves, knocked the poker from the man's hand, and flung him to the floor. The intruder's stocky body—tumbling wildly—demolished a coffee table and rolled twice more.

Then the man scrambled back to his feet, the fireplace shovel clenched in his hand. Jonah dodged, his eyes never leaving the intruder.

Paige searched frantically for some kind of weapon to help. The movement brought attention to her, however, and with a snarling grunt, the man heaved the shovel at Jonah, then launched himself across the room toward Paige.

"Drop, Paige!" Jonah called. "To the floor!"

Paige's hand connected with the little lamp on the gateleg table in the foyer, and she threw it at the intruder's face with all her might. Then she dropped to the floor and curled up into a tight fetal ball.

Something trod on her foot, then pounding footsteps hurtled down the hall. Paige did not lift her head as she heard Jonah go past in deadly pursuit.

The sound of breaking glass echoed back down the hallway, then silence descended. Paige tried to swallow, but her throat muscles clenched. She sensed a presence above her. Gentle fingers touched her hair, then lifted her hands.

"You can get up now, love." Jonah's voice was soft, but laced with frustration. "The bugger got away."

CHAPTER 2

It was almost dark; evening shadows invaded the uneasy peace of Professor Kittridge's study. Every light in the room had been turned on to provide at least an illusion of brightness and security.

Jonah slouched deeper in the professor's favorite over-stuffed easy chair, letting the clipboard and pen slide with a soft plop to the rug. His thumb and index finger idly stroked the corners of his moustache as he watched Paige dart back through the room with her arms full of another stack of papers. She carefully placed them on the floor beside the desk where she and Kittridge had been working the past four hours.

"That's enough for now, girl," the professor muttered gruffly without looking up. "My eyes are wearing out."

"Let me take over for awhile then," Paige offered for the third time. "You can cross-check the papers I'm uncertain about tomorrow."

Jonah watched Kittridge throw down a stack of index cards and lift his head to glare at Paige. With his shock of white hair flying askew and the gold wire-rimmed glasses slipping on his nose, he reminded Jonah of a clean shaven Mark Twain.

"If you don't give it a rest, I'll have Jonah chase you down and use some of his fancy *kung fu* moves on *you!*" he roared with the irascibility of an old grizzly.

They both glanced across at Jonah; his mouth quirked. "It wasn't *kung fu*," he said mildly, patting his shirt pocket, then his slacks.

"You put them on the table beside you," Paige told him automatically.

Jonah turned, retrieved his glasses, and put them on. Rising, he strolled toward the drooping woman fighting so hard to hide her exhaustion. "Why don't we all go out for a bite? It's almost seven-thirty," he suggested, stopping a few feet from Paige.

She was composed but still too pale. The freckles scattered across her long narrow nose stood out like tiny spatters of mud, and the gray eyes were shadowed with fatigue and remnants of shocked disbelief.

But at least she had quit trembling. Jonah glanced at her left leg—it was still now. When he raised his gaze back to her face, Paige was watching, chin lifted and lips pressed tightly together. Jonah sighed inwardly. For a few incredible moments this morning, his reserved, quintessentially professional research assistant had been delightfully addled. She'd also been confusing: *Why on earth had she apologized for the mess in the house?*

He turned to Kittridge so Paige's spine wouldn't shatter. She seemed so brittle. Later, over dinner, when they were in different surroundings, maybe he could distract her. Only the Lord knew how much *she* distracted him! His arms still remembered how her soft, slender form had felt when she collapsed against him, the short, silky, moonbeam-colored strands of her hair spilling across his chest. He stuffed his hands in his pockets as if the tingling sensation were visible. He knew—had known for weeks—that if Paige caught even a hint of his deepening feelings for her, he'd lose the best research assistant he'd ever had.

"I've got a few things I want to check in the 'Nam room," Kittridge abruptly announced. He stood, glancing from Jonah to Paige, then back to Jonah. "You two go on—bring me a doggie bag."

The professor's heavy-handed matchmaking infuriated Paige and amused Jonah. "If you're sure. . ." Jonah murmured dryly. His gaze narrowed. Why did Kittridge suddenly look so—so furtive, almost?

"No!" Paige contradicted with surprising force. "We finished straightening that room. I even doublechecked when you were working on the P.O.W. files. There's no need for you to worry about it anymore tonight."

Diverted, Jonah lifted an inquiring brow. "Relax, Paige—I promise I'll bring him more than a doggie bag."

She glared at him, twisting with almost savage nervousness the cameo ring she wore. "I don't think he should stay here alone," she finally admitted. Her gaze skittered between both men. "The police said the intruder must have known his routine, or he never would have broken in at the hour he did."

"What is it, Professor?" Jonah asked, keeping his voice easy, matter-of-fact at the slight start Kittridge had been unable to conceal at Paige's words. Throughout the tediously painstaking interview with the police that morning, his emotions had reflected only anger, outrage over the destruction—and a-musement at Paige's incredulous account of Jonah's actions. He agreed without hesitation that the motive had been robbery, the trashing of his rooms a vindictive retribution for the lack of money, stereo equipment, or other valuables.

So why the shifting evasiveness of his eyes now? Why the uneasiness?

"Bah!" Kittridge stomped over and snatched up Paige's purse. "Here." He thrust it into her arms. "The two of you get out of here and quit treating me like an incompetent old man." He winked at Jonah. "Even if I am."

"I'm sorry about disrupting your research," Paige apologized stiffly while they ate. "I'll find and collate the rest of Professor

K's personal notes on the dissolution of the Gestapo tomorrow. I just gave you the ones I happened on when we were cleaning up. In the confusion I'm sure I missed some. We'll still probably have to go back to the Library of Congress, though . . . ."

Her voice faltered into silence when Jonah put down his fork, braced his hands, and leaned over the table. "I've told you it's all right," he enunciated with crisp Oxford precision. "Will you relax about it? I'm not half as concerned about the research for my book as I am about you skewering yourself on the prongs of your over-developed sense of personal responsibility!"

He grabbed his water glass and emptied it, then grimaced an apology across the table. He knew—although she had never said anything—that Paige harbored a deep-seated abhorrence for any kind of confrontation.

To soothe over the awkward moment, he decided to bring up their discovery of the previous week. "To be honest, I've been thinking of altering the plot anyway. Remember our own mystery behind the ribbons on Major Pettigrew's uniform?"

Paige relaxed a little, her lips softening into a smile. "It is exciting," she agreed. "I've imagined all sorts of theories myself, and I'm not even a writer. A mysterious list of names, hidden for almost half a century. A key. . ." She colored a little. "I guess I've speculated more than I ought to."

Jonah settled back, satisfied. "I know what you mean. I'd enjoy tracing those nine names, too." He shrugged, spreading his hands. "But there's this contract I signed. . . ."

"I'm convinced the key is to a diary. My younger sister Katy used to keep one."

The waiter appeared at their table to ask if they wanted dessert, and Jonah unobtrusively studied Paige, alternately captivated and irritated by her elusive personality. It was, he mused with an inward smile, like trying to capture moonlight on water.

Over dessert they exchanged ideas concerning the "Major Pettigrew" mystery, allowing the trauma at the professor's house to recede even more. Jonah found himself seriously considering changing his plot. His editor might kick up a fuss at the inevitable delay, but one of the perks of a world-wide reputation in both the Christian and commercial markets from eight best-sellers and a TV mini-series was having almost unlimited creative freedom.

He'd pray about it. The plot he'd been researching for six months now on both sides of the Atlantic was first-rate, and he was pleased with it. But for some reason, God in His wisdom had seen fit to place in his hands the uniform of a World War II major killed in action. Paige had discovered, concealed behind the ribbons bar, a tiny key—and a list of nine names. Why were they there? Who were the people? Jonah felt the restlessness taking hold, the surge of adrenalin that signaled the unfolding intricacies of a boundless imagination.

"Ready to go?" he asked suddenly, wanting to be alone, wanting to toy around with ideas, scribble down some plot threads. Hopefully he wouldn't have to chuck entirely the reformed Gestapo agent who teamed with a renegade Resistance hero. On the other hand, his mother always told him that nimble minds never refused to seize possible advantages of alternative situations.

Maybe the vandalizing of the professor's home hadn't been the day's waste of time Paige felt so guilty about—the Lord had used stranger devices to get his attention over the last fifteen years.

So I'll pray, Lord—and see where you lead me.

"It wasn't there, I told you. . . .Don't worry—I fixed it so there's

no way they'd know what I was after. And they can't ID me. Whaddya take me for?"

The voice on the other end of the phone iced over with contempt. "I took you for a person who could get the job done without bringing the entire Metro police force breathing down your neck."

The man rubbed sweating palms on his slacks. "I got away. They got nothin'. Nothin'!"

"Neither did you." The rebuke stung, but the coldly spoken threat that followed promised more than just a sting. "I want to know how much he's found out. Then I want him eliminated. And I want it done—soon. I can't afford to risk the slightest hint of scandal."

"He's got more papers and junk than the city dump. I can't just—"

"You have one week. Find the damaging information Professor Kittridge intimated he's been gathering in the course of his re-search—destroy it. . .and the man."

He swallowed, his Adam's apple bobbing up and down. This job wasn't the cakewalk he'd thought it would be. "What about the woman and that British writer?"

"If necessary, they will be eliminated as well. But only when I say so."

"I asked around—that Limey's a big noise—not just a two-bit hack writer. It'll take me awhile to arrange things. . . ."

"I'm not interested in excuses. If you can't do the job, I'll find somebody else." The biting voice softened, the latent threat even more unnerving. "I can arrange for anything I want. Don't become one of the things I must. . .arrange."

CHAPTER 3

Paige had just finished cross-checking some sources in the World War II room in Professor K's home when Jonah called the next morning. Instead of meeting him at the National Archives at two, he wanted Paige to meet him at the airport so they could fly down to Georgia.

"Can you be at National at—" Paige heard the sound of rustling paper, "—12:45? I've booked us on a 1:30 flight. Gate 19 A. I'll clear it with the professor."

Twelve-forty-five! That gave her less than three hours—what did he think she was, anyway? Paige stood straighter. He thought she was a "top-drawer" assistant, that's what he thought. She wouldn't let him down; she wouldn't be inadequate for her job. At least he asked instead of ordered. Not like—

"I'll be there. How many days?" Her voice was cool, professional.

"I think two ought to do it. A local museum just had a phenomenal collection of World War II memorabilia donated. I was invited to check it out if I cared to make the trip. And you know me, right? If there's a chance—I have to peer under the stone. . . ."

What about the professor? He'll be alone. Paige squashed that thought, too. "I'll see you at the airport. I trust," she couldn't help but add dryly, "that you're aware of what the deep south

20

will be like in late August?"

"Can't be worse than the Sarawak rain forest in East Malaysia. See you soon, love." His voice softened. "And thanks."

Paige gathered all the notes, her mind a cauldron of seething emotions. Ever since she had met Jonah her life had been a roller coaster, and she didn't like it.

The professor had introduced them, dropping the bombshell of Jonah's identity with Machiavellian glee. He'd known Paige had been restless, uneasy with so much free time, and would be unable to resist the opportunity to help the world-famous J. Gregory research his next Christian thriller.

"Right now I wish I *had* resisted," Paige muttered a frazzled forty minutes later as she dashed into her apartment, flung a change of clothes in her hang-up bag, and taped a note to the neighbor's door across the hall. *Lord, you know how I feel. Yet here I am again, at the beck and call of another man, bending over backwards to please him.*

She determinedly locked her mind to the disturbing flow of thoughts. As she headed for the door, her roaming gaze snagged on the envelope with the key and list of names in one of her desk cubbyholes. She snatched it up to take with her.

When we get back, I'll have to show it to Professor K and see if any of the names ring a bell with him.

But she didn't have to wait that long. At the airport she found not only Jonah, but Professor Kittridge as well. Paige swallowed an almost choking lump of relief. *At least he'll be safe for a day or two now.* She hid the thought and her relief, tapping her foot in exasperation at the two men who right now looked like a pair of truculent roosters.

"I've got legitimate research there." Professor K snapped with a fierce scowl, daring Paige to comment. "I'll stay out of your way."

"It's not that," Jonah repeated with elaborate patience, but the words were clipped, his hands jammed deep in the back pockets of his slacks. "It's that interview you told me you'd finally arranged after trying for two months. You'll miss it if you come along."

"It can wait." The professor wiped the back of his hand over his mouth. The gnarled fingers were trembling. "It can wait," he repeated, "but this other can't . . . ." His voice trailed away, and he abruptly turned his back.

Their flight was called before either of them could question him. Paige and Jonah exchanged looks, then boarded the plane in silence. The flight to Atlanta was uneventful, and Jonah rented a car to drive them two hours south to the town of Warner Robins.

Professor K slept the entire drive, but it was a restless, somehow uneasy sleep. More than once Paige twisted to watch him in concern. He kept muttering unintelligible words.

"I think he's afraid and won't admit it," Paige finally commented, unable to hide her worry. "He's seventy-two, after all. He wouldn't have stood a chance against the miserable punk who trashed the place."

"I know," Jonah soberly agreed. "I'm glad he's along—but I don't know if I can agree that it's just fear. He took the break-in with remarkable aplomb." He paused. "But something's certainly weighing on his mind. . . ."

"Do you think he really has some people to see, or was that just an excuse?"

"Wish I had my Harley," Jonah muttered, passing two cars and a slow-moving camper before replying. "I don't know," he finally answered Paige. He frowned, slid a quick glance across, then seemed to reach some inner decision.

"All I *do* know," he said slowly, thoughtfully, "is when I stopped by his office and told him where we were headed, he started as if I'd burned him with a hot poker. He mumbled something about coincidence and predestination—and informed me that he was coming along. Nothing I said could change his mind."

Paige looked unseeingly out the window. That in itself made her uneasy. Jonah in a persuasive mood could charm knotholes out of a pine tree. "That was all? No names or places? I've been working with him pretty closely on that P.O.W. book, remember. We've been updating it by adding comparisons of P.O.W.'s from Vietnam with those of Korea and World War II. If he mentioned anyone, I might know the name."

"We'll try pushing a little harder tonight. But you know what a stubborn, opinionated old rascal he is. We might not get anywhere."

Paige twisted to gaze down again at the professor's sleeping form. "He's never liked his right hand to know what the left is doing. I worked with him before I married, you know." She glanced quickly across at Jonah's impassive face, then away, wondering why she was telling him. "After my husband died, Professor K insisted on giving me a job as his research assistant." She paused. "He knew I wasn't ready for my old job at the Smithsonian, but he never has told me how—. Anyway, it had been four years—but he hadn't changed a bit. He still hasn't." She fiddled with a strand of hair. "I just hope he's not in trouble."

Jonah's arm slid across the seat, coiling around her shoulders to give her a brief hug. For a horrifying moment Paige yearned toward that quiet, Gibraltar-sized strength. Then she stiffened and kept her face averted. She felt Jonah's fingers flick through the hair covering her ear, heard a soft chuckle.

"Worry, little *koneko*, is non-productive, remember? Leave the professor in the Lord's capable hands and enjoy the trip."

Paige shot him a fulminating glare, which he serenely ignored. Every time he called her one of those foreign names,

23

she wanted to stuff the teasing words back in his too amiable face. It was obvious they were some form of endearment, but thus far Jonah refused to translate any of them. Paige never pushed, too afraid of her deepest suspicions. And fears.

The next forty-eight hours passed in a blur of old uniforms, medals, personal and official documents, maps, photographs, and yellowing newspapers. Paige and Jonah stayed too busy to worry about the activities of Professor Kittridge overmuch, although Paige could not completely shrug aside an underlying anxiety.

The first day he'd disappeared in the rental car, and they didn't even see him until breakfast the next morning. He'd been morose, abstracted, almost depressed. Paige tried to divert him from his abnormal disquiet by showing him the key and the list of names she and Jonah had discovered.

For some reason, sharing their almost fifty-year-old mystery only made the professor behave more erratically. He stared at the list of names as if holding a serpent.

"I don't believe it," he exclaimed, then closed up like the door to a bank vault. He insisted on dropping them at the museum so he could have the car again and started to leave. Then, almost as an irritable afterthought, he growled out that he'd meet them at the motel.

Paige watched the car barrel down the street, quietly stewing until Jonah walked right up to her and clasped both her clenched hands. "Let it go," he ordered gently. "He's chasing rabbits, probably. You know how eccentric he is. But I have a book to write—and I need your valuable—undistracted— assistance."

So Paige resumed work with her normal methodical dedication. But she couldn't quite still the persistent, nagging uneasiness.

The professor met them back at the museum late in the

afternoon. He refused to talk at all beyond a terse declaration that he didn't feel like talking. Their flight back to Washington was uneventful; Professor K pretended to sleep. Paige talked quietly with Jonah or read a magazine, but every so often her eyes slid to the rumpled-looking professor.

"I had to call, even though I know how you feel about me. You can heed the warning—or ignore it. I don't know how he found my address, but that professor is the kind of man who isn't going to just let the matter rest."

"Your warning isn't needed. The professor is being taken care of. I learned long ago how easy it is to get away with anything—if you have the position and the power. Even murder." The voice dropped. "I'm just following your sterling example."

An awkward pause hovered on the line. "I'm sure you can arrange—and have—anything without a qualm. You always were a vengeful child."

"And the son of a traitor who never got caught. Don't forget that, old man. If you want to pass out judgment, start with yourself."

"Your mother—"

"—Is a social-climbing snob who closes her eyes and turns her back on the unpleasant smells. But that's not the way to get it done—is it? And there's too much at stake for me to suffer from any of your belated attacks of morality. So I'll have the nosy professor taken care of—and anyone else who starts digging skeletons out of the family closet."

"That's what I'm afraid of."

A sinister laugh floated ghost-like over the line. The click and subsequent dial tone buzzed harshly. After a moment, the old man hung the phone up. His hand was trembling.

CHAPTER 4

The rhythmic ticking of the ceiling fan sounded irritatingly loud in the tense silence of Emil Kittridge's living room. The revolving paddles generated a welcome breeze, but the professor was too engrossed to notice the enervating humidity.

He reached for another handful of peanuts without taking his eyes off the notes he was reading. Suddenly he sat up straight, a sense of urgency surging through him. A ferocious frown deepened. He took off his glasses, rubbed his burning eyes, then crammed the bifocals back on his nose.

It all fit. Thanks to the timely trip to Georgia, he could document all the evidence now—he'd been able to corroborate the P.O.W.'s story. Two witnesses, wasn't that what the Bible required? Well, he'd found them. And if his suspicions were correct, the whole *family* carried a legacy of treason and unprincipled amorality.

If God really was a just God like Jonah insisted, maybe He'd decided to use a bulldog of an old man as His instrument of justice. He was going to have to do something about the whole mess soon—election campaigns were already under way.

Outside, something rustled the crepe myrtle under his picture window, causing the branches to scrape the side of the house. A dull thump followed, and the professor jerked upright, tearing a corner off the paper he was holding.

The neighbor's cat yowled in warning, and the air filled with the muffled screams of a cat fight.

Disgusted, Kittridge shoved back from the desk and stomped over to draw the curtains. Walking back to the untidy desk, he stood for a long time, indecision warring with anxiety.

Finally, feeling like a doddering old woman, he tore the last page out of the notebook. His gaze moved over the room, assessing, discarding hiding places. He made his way from one end of the house to the other, and at last chose what he felt was the best location. If this information was what they'd been after, it would be safe enough here, especially if his suspicions were correct and they'd already searched the house.

First thing tomorrow he'd talk to Paige and Jonah, show them the notes, and discuss how to proceed. He was too old, too slow now, to finish this one on his own. Resigned to his decision, and his ridiculous melodrama, he plodded to the kitchen, abruptly feeling every one of his seventy-two years.

He sipped hot cocoa in silence, settling into his favorite easy chair and munching the last of the peanuts. Gradually the ache in his bones receded, and a little of the tension drained. It was late. He'd go to bed and face tomorrow when it came.

He woke in the pre-dawn hours, so abruptly and so completely that a wave of goosebumps peppered his skin. He sat up, feeling his chest tightening into a painful cramp again. He could hear his heart pounding in his eardrums.

Had that been a noise *inside* the house?

Slowly, he shoved aside the sheet and stood, his hand snagging the flashlight he kept on the floor by his bed. His knees cracked with stiffness as he crept out into the hall, and he bemoaned both age and his old-maid apprehension.

Down the hall—a shadow moved. Fighting a sudden onslaught of terror, he calculated the time it would take to get to the phone on the bedside table. Creeping like an infirm old mouse, he edged backward, never taking his eyes off the shadow. It didn't move—it was just a shadow after all.

Relieved, he lowered the flashlight. Then, the corner of his eye caught a blur of movement—from the other direction.

The blow crashed into the side of his neck. Pain exploded behind his eyes, sending dazzling light swirling down a long, undulating tunnel. He knew he was falling, and then—nothing.

"...And although no man can ever predict the hour, we can rest in the knowledge that our heavenly Father has a place for us if we put our hope in His Son Jesus. Let us cling to that hope, and the peace He offers even in the midst of our grief. . . ."

Paige sat, still and cold as the gravestones surrounding them, her eyes wide, unblinking. Jonah sat beside her, holding her hand in his lap. She didn't even know when he'd taken it.

The people around her blurred; the minister's words ran together, and she tumbled unwillingly back into the past. Images flashed through her mind, the scenes roaring by as if viewed through the window of a fast-moving train. Guilt. . . pain. . . fear—all washed over her in a red tide.

"Paige?"

She looked numbly up at Jonah, then around. The service was over. Friends and acquaintances surrounded them, offering condolences and snippets of the professor's long and colorful life, murmuring that he'd died as he would have preferred it. On the way to work. Quick—mercifully quick. The minister patted her shoulder.

Finally they could go. "I want to go back to his house for a few minutes," Paige said in a lifeless monotone. She stared up at Jonah, part of her mind observing that his face was full of concern. She knew she looked like a wax figurine. Black was not her best color.

There was a moment of silence, then Jonah cupped her elbow. "All right," he said, helping her gently into the back of the limousine.

The house felt eerily empty, as if somehow it knew that its very heartbeat had been stilled. For the first time since the police had called her three days ago, Paige felt tears sting her eyes. Behind her, Jonah quietly shut the door and turned on the hall light. Paige stared at the coat rack, two hot tears sliding down her cold cheeks as she lifted her hand to stroke the professor's cane, his crushed, ancient fedora.

Surely if they took a couple of steps into the living room, he'd be there in his easy chair, munching peanuts.

Something clicked in Paige's brain. She froze, tears drying up, struggling for the thought to complete itself.

"Let's leave—this is too soon for you."

"Wait." She looked frantically around the foyer, her fingers suddenly digging into his arm. "Jonah—there's something wrong here."

She closed her eyes, trying to concentrate. She felt Jonah's hand cover her clutching fingers, but all her energy was directed to capturing that elusive sensation. She would distance herself from Jonah when she had the answer.

When it hit her, she swayed.

"Jonah. . ." her voice shook. "Jonah, the police said the professor was found at the Metro station he usually takes."

"That's correct." His tone was patient. "He wasn't attacked, love—there were no signs of struggle—his briefcase was even still by him. The heart attack must have been sudden. The bruise on his neck came from hitting the concrete abutment when he fell. Paige—" He took her arms, gave her a gentle shake. "It's okay to cry. You don't—"

She tore herself free. "Jonah—I'm trying to tell you! That can't be right. He uses—used—the Metro, and I know he had high blood pressure—but he didn't go there the morning he died!"

Her teeth were practically chattering now from the terrifying realization. "Jonah—Professor K was murdered."

CHAPTER 5

Paige rubbed the back of her neck, wincing at the combined irritants of muscle fatigue and a headache. Glancing at her watch, she was astonished to see that it was almost five. She'd been searching through Professor K's papers over seven hours now.

Seven hours today. Twenty or so over the previous two days, futilely presenting her case to Jonah and the police.

"Sure, something had been bothering him—his health. Everyone noticed."

"Forgetting his cane and fedora—no matter how entrenched in habit he might have been—does not constitute enough evidence to initiate a homicide investigation, Ms. Hawthorne. There's nothing, remember, to indicate that break-in earlier this week had any motive beyond vandalism."

"There's a good possibility it precipitated the heart attack, but that's the only connection."

"He was probably already slightly disoriented before he left the house, Paige. It's a miracle he didn't crash his car on the way to the station."

Everyone had been patient. Everyone had been gentle and polite. But in the end, everyone had been patronizing. Paige quit arguing—and her determination hardened.

She stood, did a few bend and stretch exercises to relax her muscles, then sat back down. Should she work a little longer, risk facing the quiet censure in a pair of midnight blue eyes?

Jonah, she knew, was sure to do more than merely raise a censorious eyebrow this time. Or at least he would if he finished his business in New York and could catch a hop back to D.C. today. The urgent call from his editor that morning had sent him off to National on his Harley-Davidson an hour later.

Paige surveyed the neatly organized mounds of paperwork surrounding her and half smiled. Before he left, muttering some ominous sounding foreign words directed toward editor and publisher, Jonah had tried to extract a promise from her to take the day off from work.

"Relax—go visit your old chums at the Smithsonian or something. Forget my book, and forget your theories about the professor, Paige. You're wound tighter than a sailor's knot in hurricane winds."

She abruptly stood back up, forcing aside her thoughts. She decided to take a break before she tackled the nightstand in the professor's bedroom. Something, somewhere in the house had to yield a clue, and then Jonah and the police would place more credence in her absolute conviction that Emil Kittridge had been murdered.

"But why? *Why?*" she demanded aloud. The question—still unanswered—bounced off indifferent walls.

Her red-rimmed gaze fell almost haphazardly on the protruding corner of a notebook sandwiched between two books on the Vietnam war. Out of sheer habit and her compulsive tidiness, Paige reached out to align the notebook with the two volumes. The spiral caught, and Paige tugged the notebook out.

It was a smaller notebook than Professor K usually used—

about five-by-seven. Paige leafed through it, noting that most of the information dealt with the Vietnam era, which was probably why it had been left with those two books. *Clever, Paige. You're a regular Sherlock Holmes.* Some pages had been torn out of the back.

Curiosity battled with exhaustion as she sank down into the chair again, pinching the bridge of her nose as her burning eyes struggled to decipher the professor's sprawling script. "1965-68" had been neatly inscribed across the top; pages were subdivided by subject: battles, military references, and the like. Below were names of men, the date the professor had visited them, and the coding system referring to the professor's files. He had been, she thought with painful wistfulness, *such* a fanatic for organization—a lot of her own research habits were directly attributable to Professor Kittridge's insistence that she "document, document, document!"

At first, a name added to the bottom of a page didn't register because her mind was dulled by exhaustion and a sudden onslaught of painful memories. "James D—" The writing looked hurried, almost scribbled. "—Med-der, Georgia?" Paige mumbled—and awareness slapped her in the face at last. "Georgia. *Georgia?*"

Was this one of the people Professor Kittridge had visited when he had insisted on flying down with them? If so, and she talked to this person, maybe she could find a reason for the professor's odd behavior those two days. She glared at the wispy fragments of paper clinging to the spirals at the bottom of the notebook. At least one other page had been ripped out. Why had he done that?

Paige tossed the notebook down, and spent a fruitless ten minutes flipping through the two Vietnam books, hoping he'd absentmindedly used the notes to mark pertinent pages or something. But that would be so unlike him—he used paper-clips, not scraps of paper, to mark pages.

Nothing. There was nothing.

Could he have thrown the page away? Shaking her head in instant denial, Paige had to acknowledge Professor K would not have done that either. He never threw *anything* away, including empty peanut jars. He had a shed out back filled with them, as well as yellowing newspapers, worn out shoes, and rusting lawn tools.

That only left one alternative. He'd ripped the page or pages out for the express purpose of placing them somewhere else. She searched rapidly through the piles of notebooks and index cards once more, just to be sure. Suspicions mounting, she ran back to the Vietnam room. The files seemed to be in order, and yet. . . .

Paige straightened slowly, comprehension surging through her in a rising tide. She sank down in the chair next to the library desk. "He must have suspected," she whispered out-loud. "He must have known. . . ." Lifting her head to the ceiling, eyes wet, she clenched her hands into fists. "Father, why didn't he share with me? Why didn't he ask for help?"

Her head dropped and she buried her face in her hands. "Why did you let him die?"

After awhile, she pushed back in the chair, sat up, and drew a deep determined breath. Rising, she marched for the kitchen to buoy her body and spirit with some of the leftovers from the funeral. She had a lot to do.

CHAPTER 6

Slipping in and out of the heavy traffic, Jonah maneuvered the Harley with almost reckless skill. Beneath the visored helmet, his face was lined with fatigue and grimness.

Paige hadn't been at her apartment, which left him with one unpleasant alternative; he knew she hadn't just trotted out to enjoy a leisurely meal in a restaurant. The only time she ever ate out instead of cooking a meal had been when Jonah or the professor insisted.

The professor.

She was going to kill herself over her dogged notion that he had been murdered. Mouth flattening into a thin line of determination, Jonah gunned the Harley past a slow moving car and darted in front of a silver BMW, then sped down the exit ramp.

It was almost seven o'clock when he turned onto the tree-lined street where Kittridge had lived. Twilight cast lengthening purple shadows; the incessant roar of freeway traffic faded. The only noise came from the muted sputtering of the engine of his modified Harley. It should have been an atmosphere of pastoral tranquility. Should have been.

Jonah pulled into the driveway, killed the engine, and stared at the house. Every window blazed with light—Paige hadn't

34

even drawn the shades. Yanking his gloves off and tossing them in his helmet, he ran lightly up the steps.

She hadn't locked the front door, either, and Jonah decided with the rashness of exhaustion to teach her an obviously needed lesson. Apparently the intruder the other day hadn't been enough.

She was in the Vietnam room, crouched down on hands and knees with her back to the doorway. He tiptoed over until he was standing just behind her.

"Now if I'd been a burglar or—"

The words died abruptly when Paige jerked as if jabbed with a hot needle, then leapt to her feet to face an astonished Jonah. A butcher knife was clenched in her right hand, poised for attack.

They stared at one another for an endless span of seconds before Jonah reached out and very gently, very carefully removed the knife from her upraised hand. "I can see," he murmured, "that I was misled by the carelessness of open windows and unlocked doors. Sneaking up on you could be dangerous." He tossed the knife in the air, catching it by the handle before absently tossing it again while he watched Paige. "It's certainly an improvement over the last time I startled you, but isn't it a trifle risky, tempting circumstances like this?"

Paige's complexion changed from the white of a Suffolk sheep to sunset red. "How could you *do* that to me? You know I—" She stopped, hands automatically lifting to check her hair. "You're lucky I didn't have the courage to attack."

"Well, now, I could return with a 'you're lucky I didn't have to defend against your attack'." He watched embarrassment and frustration war with anger. Relieved but still irritated about the windows and door, he hefted the knife in his hands one last time. He tested the blade with his thumb, then laid it on the floor. "You should have at least locked the door."

"Why? If the murderer wants to have a go at me as well, he'd

35

just break a window." She paused, her look both defiant and fragile. "Professor K didn't die of a stroke or a heart attack, Jonah." She picked up a small spiral notebook and thrust it at him. "I found this—one or more pages have been torn out of the back. And that's not the only thing."

Jonah flipped through the notebook, then lifted his gaze back to Paige. "So?"

"I've known—" Her voice thickened, then settled into flatness, "—knew—the professor for ten years. He never threw anything away. Not even candy wrappers. It drove his maid crazy. And, Jonah—I can't even *find* his Vietnam notebooks."

"Umph." As an answer, he knew it wasn't much, but it had been useless to argue with Paige lately. Jonah scratched his forehead, fiddled with his moustache, covertly studying her. She was passionately convinced of her theory, to the point he better do more than merely humor her. "So this notebook you *did* find—you think he deliberately tore out some sheets, then?"

Paige nodded eagerly. "Yes! Don't you see? He *hid* them—they must have been some sort of clue as to why he was murdered. Jonah, you *have* to see. . . ."

From outside the window a plaintive meow broke the night. Paige jumped, and Jonah was on his feet, poised protectively in front of her before the sound faded. Claws scratched the screen, and the cat meowed again. Jonah and Paige looked at each other, then burst into sheepish laughter.

"Jasper." Paige shook her head, walking over to the window. "He's so spoiled. . . ."

She opened the window, unhooked the screen, and the neighbor's gigantic orange tom jumped with an inelegant thud onto the floor. After wrapping himself around Paige's leg, he strolled out the door and headed for the pantry, his tail gently waving with pleasure.

"Professor K got him hooked on boiled peanuts." Paige

blinked furiously, her smile wobbling. "I don't know what will happen now that—"

A series of thumps, clattering, and breaking glass erupted from the opposite end of the house.

"Oh, no. . ." Paige started for the door. "He's probably gotten into the pantry. I shouldn't have—"

Jonah caught her arm. "I'll go get the beastie. You start cleaning up, and I'll take you out for a spot of supper." He tried his most persuasive grin. "I'm beat from my trek to the Big Apple."

"I can make something."

"I know, but I'd like to take you out." His fingers brushed her cheekbone. "Please. . ."

"I—all right." She glanced around. "I'll clean up. Don't be angry at Jasper, Jonah. He can't help it if he's clumsy and spoiled."

"That's something you wouldn't know about, isn't it?" Jonah murmured as he left. "Don't worry!" he called back over his shoulder. "I won't hurt the cat."

CHAPTER 7

He returned some moments later, holding Jasper in his arms and scratching the purring tom's ears and neck. The cat kneaded his paws on Jonah's forearm, looking disgustingly oblivious to the fact that Jonah had just spent the past ten minutes cleaning up the mess he'd made of the pantry.

"I—uh—brought him back here. Maybe we should let him exit the way he came."

"Probably." Paige was studying him with a frown between her eyes. She opened her mouth as if to speak, shut it, then shrugged irritably and blurted, "Jonah, when Jasper meowed, why did you jump in front of me like that?"

"Mm. . .instinct, I suppose." He reopened the screen and gently shoved a reluctant Jasper out the window. "I spent a rather interesting summer in Bangladesh once—still tend to react. . .off the cuff, shall we say, when I'm startled."

Jonah faced the fact that he was stalling. He watched Jasper settle on the grass to fastidiously clean his left hind leg and tried to think of a way to drop a lighted match into a pool of petrol without having everything explode.

"Jonah, what are you not telling me?"

Sometimes he wished the woman wasn't so infernally astute. Sighing, he turned around, and with reluctant fingers reached into his hip pocket and tugged out a sheet of notebook paper.

It had been folded many times, into a tight little square. "I found this on the floor in the remains of one of the jars friend Jasper broke." He paused, then added roughly, "I'm afraid you might be right about the professor's death, Paige. I'm sorry."

She stared at him in stunned silence, then reached shaking fingers for the paper. Jonah watched as she carefully opened, then read it, awareness and growing horror spreading over her face. "He really was murdered," she said numbly. "Wasn't he . . . ."

Jonah lifted the notes out of her hand. "There does seem to be more of a likelihood now. He was certainly eccentric, but not even the professor would have done something like this—" he fanned the paper in the air, "—unless he felt like he'd found some sort of pretty damaging evidence. What I don't understand is why he didn't talk to us, share whatever it was that was making him so nervous, so suspicious."

"Somebody killed him."

Jonah glanced sharply at her. She was trembling, her eyes staring sightlessly, lips quivering in a dead white face. "Paige—" he laid his hand on her shoulder.

She jerked away. "Leave me alone." She turned blindly, then slumped, her arms crossing over her stomach as if she were in deep pain.

Jonah stuffed the notes back in his pocket and reached for her. At first she only suffered the embrace, her body stiff. But when he forced her head to his shoulder, she finally gave in and held him, just held him, her hands clinging to his shirt.

They sat in the breakfast nook of Paige's apartment, the supper remains shoved to one side of the table. Paige had adamantly insisted on cooking the meal, needing on a deep subconscious level to show her competence at *something*.

Jonah had argued, then looked closely into her face, and

39

given in. He hadn't let her clean up, however. Paige, exhausted enough to concede, allowed him to stack the dishes and push them aside so they could talk. The piece of paper lay opened in front of them.

"A family," Paige muttered. She felt as if someone had poured mud in her brain. " '*Has* to be same family,' he says. But what family?"

Jonah leaned back, lacing his hands behind his head. He looked at the ceiling and quoted the scrawled, cryptic phrase that was driving them both crazy. " 'Too much to be coincidence. Has to be the same family. Bad blood—sins of the fathers. . .' Why couldn't he have been more specific?"

"I told you," Paige repeatedly tiredly. "He was like that. If he discovered something really bad about an individual, he had to be careful—even with researched documentation—about what he put on paper. He told me once that one lawsuit for slander was one too many. And I know that's why he hid the paper instead of talking about it. He'd want to verify all his facts first."

"Mmph," Jonah grunted. "We could take this all to the police, but I wonder. . ." he shrugged, looking strangely helpless all of a sudden.

Paige swallowed, then twined her fingers together in her lap so Jonah wouldn't see their shaking. "I know. But I can't just let it die."

"Neither can I." He shoved away from the table suddenly and surged to his feet. "Neither can I." The glitter in his darkening eyes reminded Paige uneasily of lightning in storm clouds. "The professor must have gotten too close, because someone was willing to commit murder to prevent him from investigating futher. And that—" he finished grimly, "—means they're ready to do it again."

Paige paled but added, "It has to tie in to that list of names I showed him. I know you think I'm stretching it, but it's all we have to go on until I get back over to his house, look up the codes, and hunt down the rest of his Vietnam notes."

"You're not to go there alone."

She shriveled inside; the instinct to submit to the order was so overpowering she almost caved in. "I don't want to," she admitted, avoiding his eyes, "but I'm the only one who knows the code to his files. He never even told his personal secretary. If you want to join me, fine. But I'm going over there."

Jonah folded his arms across his chest and shook his head, his mouth beneath the bristly moustache a thin, unsmiling line.

Paige jumped up and began clearing the table. *It's happening again, Lord. I'm letting it happen again.* "I'll just straighten the kitchen first. Do you want the leftovers? Maybe I should take them to Jasper."

"Paige."

She stopped, her back to Jonah. He didn't make a sound, but she felt his approach with every quivering nerve in her body.

"Don't go over there tonight. Please."

He was right behind her, but he didn't touch her. Ashamed, defiant, frightened, Paige turned around. "I have to," she muttered miserably. "I won't be able to sleep anyway." She tried to hide her turmoil, but must have been unsuccessful, for Jonah's expression softened.

"All right. All right, love." He hesitated, then asked, "Why did you cringe from me, Paige?" The look in the midnight blue eyes was indescribable. "That's not the first time, either. What have I ever done to make you afraid of me?"

"I'm not afraid of you," Paige shot back automatically. She busied herself with dumping leftovers in plastic storage containers. "I'm not afraid," she repeated, knowing that it wasn't entirely true. "I just don't like to be ordered around as if I were a puppet or a three-year-old child."

41

Jonah helped her clean up, his movements swift and economical. "Someday," he promised softly as they prepared to leave, "you're going to tell me what happened to you."

She grabbed her purse off the couch. "Don't, Jonah."

"It was your husband, wasn't it?"

Paige froze, then opened the front door, and set the lock. She turned back, flicked a brief glance upward at the impassive face. "Yes." She ground out the word, then fled down the steps.

CHAPTER 8

Jonah made Paige wait in her car with the doors locked until he conducted a thorough search of the professor's house. Paige was cravenly relieved. "Thanks," she told him after he waved an all clear and she joined him inside. "I know we might be overreacting, but. . ."

"Taking precautions while scrounging for murder clues is not—" Jonah paused, then added crisply, "—overreacting. And first thing in the morning we take all this to the police. They—we—didn't listen to you earlier, but things have changed."

Paige gnawed on her lip a minute, then blurted, "I'm sorry, Jonah. Sorry about it all. Your book—"

". . .Is almost at the point where I can start writing the first draft, so zip up the apologies." He pushed her toward the hall. "Step on it, love. I'd like to be out of here as soon as we can. Try to come up with something concrete enough so we won't look too melodramatic when we dump this whole affair in the laps of the local bobbies."

A reluctant smile inched across Paige's face. "Why don't you run down to the deli and grab some snacks while I get started, then? I threw out the last of the leftovers from the funeral, and I know you'll want some munchies while you wait." She smiled when Jonah ducked his head. "Go on. I'll be fine. You've

43

made sure the place in empty, and I promise I'll lock the door after you."

"You're sure?"

Paige nodded.

"I'll be back in ten minutes." He stepped out the door, then poked his head back in. "Would've been five if I had my bike instead of your car."

Paige sniffed, locked the door after him, rubbed her hands together, and went to work. The professor's filing system reflected the man: idiosyncratic, complex, and painstakingly thorough. Paige lost track of time.

A car pulled into the convenience store parking lot almost the same time Jonah did. He barely noticed because he was in too big a hurry to get back to Paige. He didn't like leaving her, but knew making an issue of the matter would have backed Paige into yet another corner.

He grabbed half a dozen snack items without really noticing, paid for them, and dashed back out to the car. Two blocks down the street, the steering wheel jerked in his hands as the car suddenly lurched. Jonah steadied the vehicle and managed to pull over to the curb.

A puncture! Of all the times! The hot night closed around him, cloud cover obscuring the moonlight. The nearest street-lamp was a good fifty feet away. He grabbed a flashlight, flung himself out, and was yanking open the trunk when a car pulled up behind him and stopped. A suit clad man, almost invisible except for the pale blur of his face, approached.

"Need some help?"

"Thanks—I'd appreciate it. I'm in a bit of a hurry—" He stopped, his stomach muscles tightening into steel cables. Something about the man's stance. . .the shape of his body. The hand hovering at his waist as if—

Jonah dived, catching the man on his shins and knocking

him down just as he pulled a gun out from beneath his jacket. A swift sideways chop with the side of Jonah's hand stunned him enough to give Jonah time to roll backward, placing Paige's car between his body and the gun.

A car was approaching from the other direction. The gunman, who had just scrambled back to his feet, was caught directly in the glare of the headbeams. Crouched behind Paige's car, Jonah heard an expletive, then the sound of scrambling footsteps. As the approaching car passed, the gunman's car roared to life, burning rubber as it shot off down the street.

Jonah stood, shaking and sweating like a racehorse after the Grand National. He stared stupidly after the disappearing taillights until the car careened around a corner. Then, wild with fear over Paige, he raced back to the convenience store at a dead run. He'd call the professor's house as soon as he finished calling the police.

Paige had unearthed three names and addresses from the list, stacking the file folders on them in a neat pile on the library table. As she turned back to the cabinet, she glanced at her watch, and started in surprise. Almost an hour had passed. Where on earth was Jonah?

Frowning, more than a little concerned, she hesitated, feeling foolish. Jonah had chastised her more than once about assuming responsibility for someone else's actions, especially his. Then through the closed door came the faint sound of a ringing phone. Jonah! Relieved, Paige started toward the door.

A ball of fire exploded through the window, shattering the panes in a shower of glass. It landed with a roar on the library table, skittered across it and fell to the floor in a conflagration of ignited papers. Tongues of flame licked up the legs of the table, snaked across the threadbare carpet, and attacked another mound of papers. Smoke and gaseous fumes billowed, filling the room with thick, choking black smoke as the library table and more papers ignited.

Just as suddenly the lights went out, plunging the house into darkness—except for the writhing red and yellow flames.

Rigid with terror, Paige took a step toward the burning papers, then convulsed in a paroxysm of coughing as the billowing smoke engulfed her. Her eyes stung, filling with tears.

With a crackling roar, the fire shot up the drapes.

The files! The papers! Father in heaven—the papers!

She dropped to the floor, coughing and choking. She had to get the papers. A fiery tendril trailed a meandering path across the carpet toward her. Hypnotized by the almost sensuous slow motion, Paige stared at the crackling, popping ribbon until, with a sound almost like a sigh, it attacked the dried-up philodendron next to one of the old lawyer's bookcases.

Behind her, a roaring blast of heat hit her back; she scrambled around—and watched flames block her path to the door.

There was nothing she could do to save the professor's papers. Unless she acted quickly, she might not be able to save herself. Paige spared an agonizing second to renounce a lifetime of work, then began crawling toward her only hope of escape.

She couldn't see.

She couldn't breathe.

Racked with coughs, praying desperate little incoherent prayers, she crawled toward the other window in the room. Her streaming, stinging eyes strained to see past the choking smoke and flames.

I have to make it to that window, or I'm going to die. Father, is it time for me to die?

The floor was hot; her face was hot; her lungs were burning. She shuffled in the boiling red and orange darkness, cringing when the burning drapes collapsed with a crackling roar. Gathering strength, the flames engulfed the first set of filing cabinets.

Panic lashed her. The fire was closing in around her. She banged into the wall, and her hands flailed wildly, searching. Where was the window? It had to be on this wall.

She jerked her hands back. The walls were searing hot.

Another paroxysm of coughing doubled her over. She wiped a sooty hand across her burning eyes. She had to find the window. Her hand brushed against a smoother, cooler surface, and she sobbed aloud in relief.

Now to get it open. Her fingers wouldn't cooperate—where was the catch? It wouldn't budge. *I'm sorry, Professor.* Her ears flooded with the sound and fury of the roaring inferno as she thrust herself to her feet, swaying.

With the last of her strength, Paige grabbed the first object her groping hand brushed against, her fingers closing convulsively around it. She lifted her arm, staggered, then heaved with all her might.

CHAPTER 9

Paige fought a heavy suffocating shroud. *I'm not dead,* she tried to say, but fire and smoke still filled her throat. She gagged.

"Take it easy. You're okay, miss."

She had to break the window. Had to break the window. She tried to move her arms, but they were bound tightly to her sides.

Something covered her mouth, her nose. She struggled. It hurt to breathe.

"Paige! *Paige!*"

She was floating, being shaken like a rag doll, squeezed like—like—she coughed again, and pain brought her, finally, back to consciousness.

"Paige. . ." Jonah's hoarse voice broke next to her ear. Something soft brushed against her temple. Paige opened her eyes, blinking. Within the darkness his face was bathed in a blood red glow, and behind the blurred bulk of his shoulders, a wall of fire strained skyward. She tried to say his name. Her breathing labored, she heaved as she again tried to rise, to do something—save something.

"Easy—" A fireman was kneeling on her other side, a portable oxygen tank next to him. Paige finally realized there was a mask over her mouth and nose.

"Easy, ma'am. Just breathe normally."

How could she breathe normally when her lungs were on fire? He eyes and nose burned, her skin burned—and her head throbbed as if someone had taken a bat to it. But the quiet voice repeated instructions over and over, and Jonah held her still. Paige quit struggling, and concentrated on trying to breathe through the searing pain.

The night burned black and scarlet, with the throbbing roar from the fire trucks competing with the roaring crackle of the fire. Shapeless figures darted in and out of the darkness, their shouts and instructions sporadically rising above the rest of the noise.

Eventually she realized she was lying in Jonah's arms, but she was far too weak to protest. Someone had draped a blanket around her shoulders, and she clutched at it convulsively, with fingers that felt like jumbled toy blocks.

"Paige. . .love, you can relax. It's okay; you're safe."

She felt his hand stroking hers, the fingers gently prying hers open. "Jonah?" She winced. Muffled through the oxygen mask, her voice emerged in a harsh, smoke-roughened whisper. "I—I can't move my fingers."

"I know. It's okay. I know." He continued stroking, rubbing, and Paige managed to turn her head enough to see that she was clutching a solid brass bookend shaped like a pair of books. The back of her hand was covered with cuts and scratches, still oozing blood.

"I—it's the professor's. . .I had to—to—" She coughed and started to struggle. "I have to—"

It took both Jonah and the EMT to keep her down. Her eyes, still tearing, focused wildly on the holocaust in front of her. Jonah finally put his hand to the side of her face and turned it firmly aside. "There's nothing you can do, love."

"Just relax, ma'am. You've hit your head. We'll be getting

you to the hospital in a few minutes, as soon as the ambulance arrives."

Paige went limp, and she felt Jonah finally pry the bookend free of her convulsive hold. A shudder rippled down her body. She lifted her hand to touch her throbbing forehead.

"I'm a mess. I need to change—the professor's papers—I'm sorry—"

"Hush," Jonah murmured. "Hush, now. It's okay."

"Still in shock a little, I'd think," the EMT commented. His hand covered her wrist, his fingers feeling her racing pulse. "There's the ambulance now."

Paige turned her eyes toward the matter-of-fact voice. "I'm fine," she protested indistinctly. "I don't need to go to the hospital. I need to stay here. I need to talk to the police—the fire. Arson—someone threw—" She choked. It hurt to talk, but she had to tell them. "There might be something—the professor's—"

"Someone will talk to you at the hospital. Did you say her name was Paige? Someone will take your statement there, Paige." The brusque professional voice was kind but firm. "Right now you just need to lie still and relax."

"How bad do you think it is?" Jonah asked. His voice sounded strained, as if he were poised on the edge of a cliff. Paige's gaze swung back to look up into his face. He was looking at the technician, his mouth a grim slashing line. The EMT hesitated, then ticked off a blunt assessment.

"Looks like mostly superficial cuts and the blow to her head. She must have hit it when she came out the window. That's where we found her. I don't know how long she'd been unconscious. The pupil reaction's okay, so I don't think she's concussed. Some slight first degree burns. Smoke inhalation's probably the most potentially dangerous problem."

"I see." Jonah's hand drifted down to touch her forehead—so softly Paige barely felt it. "You heard what she said?"

"I heard. We'll have people investigating—"

"Investigate all you want," Jonah snapped softly. "But there was nothing accidental about that fire."

Paige gazed numbly up into his face, wondering why she'd ever thought of him as docile and easy-going. He caught her look, and in the surreal light, it looked almost like more fire had ignited behind his eyes.

"The paramedics'll be here in a minute. She can give her statement at the hospital," the emergency medical technician repeated. He sounded uncomfortable.

Why were they talking like she wasn't even here?

"I want to stay. Maybe they salvaged something. I've got to check—the files, all his work. . ." She stopped, choking, her raw vocal chords screaming in protest.

"I'll take care of it." Jonah's hand closed over her shoulder. "Try to just relax, Paige. Close your eyes."

Two men approached, wheeling a stretcher. As they lifted her, panic filled her, and she fought the constricture of blanket and oxygen mask. "Jonah—don't. . . don't. . ." She felt his hand enfold hers and immediately relaxed.

"I won't leave you, love."

They wheeled her past the burning house, and Paige turned her head aside, her eyes closed.

She had to stay overnight at the hospital for observation, but the next morning a sore throat, bruised forehead, singed hair, and skin that felt and looked sunburned were the only physical reminders of the previous night.

Throughout the entire dreary process of talking to the police, an arson investigator, and a representative from an insurance company, her emotions remained detached. They told her that not only had the fire been deliberate—but heavy traffic and a false alarm had prevented the fire department from responding any sooner. By the time they arrived, it had been too late to save anything. The police detective informed Paige that she was extremely lucky to be alive, much less relatively unharmed.

Paige calmly agreed and answered all the questions with a sort of ethereal poise. When Jonah came to pick her up, she was waiting quietly in a chair by her hospital room window, hands folded in her lap.

"It's a beautiful day. Is it real hot?"

"High eighties." He looked as if he were going to say something else, but didn't. He handed her some clothes he'd picked up from her apartment and waited out in the hall while she changed.

Instead of taking her home, Jonah drove them to a mall in Springfield. "We have to talk," he told Paige, leading her inside. He held her hand, not releasing it until they were sitting at a back corner table in one of the crowded mall cafes.

If Paige hadn't known better, she would have thought that Jonah was acting like a man who saw a threat behind every tree. Scenes of the previous night flashed into her mind, and she bit her lip. Suddenly, his elaborate precautions didn't seem so silly.

After ordering a meal neither of them wanted, Jonah studied her in silence until Paige stirred uneasily. "You've obviously brought me here for a reason, so how about letting me in on it. I promise not to dissolve in hysteria. See—" she extended her arms, displaying rock steady hands, "—no shakes. I'm fine. Fine."

Jonah waited while the waitress finished serving his coffee and some hot tea for Paige. His steady blue gaze told Paige he knew her composure was based on the anesthesia of shock. "It's not easy. . ."

"Jonah, after the past two weeks you could tell me *my* apartment was torched, and I don't think I'd care at this point." She picked up the mug of tea and glowered at it. "I feel," she

52

confessed rather truculently, "like I've stepped into one of your books."

"Your apartment wasn't torched," Jonah said, then added calmly, "it was searched and trashed just like the professor's."

The mug tilted precariously. "*What?*"

"And the reason I wasn't in the professor's house with you last night is because someone arranged for the car to have a puncture. When I got out to change it, a man tried to gun me down. It was too dark to see him clearly—but I'm pretty sure it was the same man I chased off at Professor K's. I think that's what clued me—the body shape, the way he stood. But I still didn't get a clear view of his face." He drank some coffee, his eyes never leaving Paige's. "The police have the punctured tire and are trying to run a check on all the dark blue Nissan Sentras with Maryland plates—a formidable task. Beyond that, all they could to is advise me to be extra careful—and guard my back."

He leaned across the table, his hand coming to rest on top of Paige's, which was lying limply by the forgotten tea. "So, darlin', you and I are putting my book on hold while we try our hand at solving our own mystery."

CHAPTER 10

Paige look stupefied, and Jonah couldn't blame her. He felt the same way. Eating mechanically, not tasting the food, he tried to keep his mind from returning to the previous night, when, for a few eternity-spanning moments, he'd thought she was dead.

Without any doubt, he loved her.

What do I do now, Lord? I'm in love with my research assistant.

The thought had been growing for weeks, but the depth of his feelings hadn't registered until the fire. He glanced across at her again, and in spite of his mood, a grin tugged at his mouth. She looked as fragile as a moonflower, but the blank shock had faded, and the expression on her face now could only be described as—disgruntled.

"How can you sit there so calmly, knowing that someone is out there trying to kill us—and we don't even know why?" The hoarse voice was curious rather than outraged.

Jonah's grin broadened. "How can you?"

Paige considered that a moment, then shrugged. "I don't know. . .none of it seems real." She looked down at her plate. "I don't think it's even really registered that Professor K is dead."

54

"How did you react when your husband died?"

Jonah saw a visible reaction on Paige's face as she closed right up, looking as remote and unreachable as the moon. "I think we should keep our discussion on trying to find clues."

"Paige," he kept his voice as mild as he could, "I don't think you understand." He glanced around the restaurant, feeling like a right proper Keystone cop but needing, all the same, to make sure they couldn't be overheard. "There're at least two people actively trying to murder us—because that guy acted like a professional on a job. The police are sympathetic—but unless and until we can ID someone—we're on our own. They have neither the manpower, time, or money to provide us with round-the-clock protection."

Paige looked as if she'd swallowed her spoon with her tea. Jonah winced inwardly.

"So you see. . .I need to understand you, I need to know how you're going to react to the constant threat of danger. Will you scream and cower—or attack with a butcher knife?"

Paige only looked at him. Her eyes still remote.

He stood, held her chair, and took her elbow as they threaded their way toward the cash register and out of the mall. He didn't like the distant passivity on her face or the iciness of her fingers. *We need an extra dose of your strength, Lord. . .and your protection.*

After they were in the car, Jonah locked the doors and glanced around again. "What would you think," he asked slowly, "of putting up in a hotel near my apartment building until this is over? I can't very well move into yours—and it wouldn't do much good to hide out in my place in the mountains." He thought with brief regret of the tri-level log home he had built when he took out U.S. citizenship. One day he hoped he could take Paige there, but not yet. . . .

"I guess there's not a whole lot of choice," Paige replied. She

55

swallowed with difficulty, but her voice didn't falter. "The Bergman Arms is only a couple of blocks from your apartment, isn't it? Would that do?"

"Mm. As long as they have good security."

"What about you? Is it safe for you to stay in—"

"It's Jay's apartment, remember? I'm just leasing it while he's in England. The killer wouldn't be able to look up my address because the apartment's in Jay's name."

"He could have followed you."

"No one has—yet." That thought had already occurred to him and to the police as well. He'd at least been able to assure them he could spot a tail.

"Why are you smiling?"

Jonah started the engine, then glanced across at her. "They didn't believe me down at the station when I promised I'd know if I was being followed. One of the detectives decided to see for himself."

"Well?"

"I dodged him, then came up behind him three blocks later," he admitted, albeit sheepishly. He sneaked a peek at Paige, and almost rear-ended a van. She was staring at him as if he'd sprouted two heads and was belching green smoke.

"How did—never mind, I don't want to know." She leaned back against the seat and closed her eyes, looking so fragile, his hands almost crushed the steering wheel.

He'd never realized how truly sheltered Paige was. She was articulate, intelligent, resourceful, and without doubt, an historian of the first water. She'd unearthed oddments of information that would give his book added depth, and she could charm obdurate old ladies out of a half-century worth of family papers.

But she was also, from the little Professor K had shared, a home-and-hearth Kansas farm girl whose greatest adventure had been the move to D.C., away from her family.

Nothing in her life had ever prepared her to cope with physical violence.

He suddenly remembered her husband, and beneath the moustache his lips thinned into a straight line. One day soon, they *were* going to have a little talk.

A century old hotel hidden in the middle of Georgetown, the Bergman Arms catered to people in all walks of life, from wealthy, aged widows, to pinstripe-suited businessmen, to the never-ending flow of tourists. Gleaming brass fixtures and oiled oak trim polished to a dull sheen over the decades attested to the low-key elegance. The faded but still rich burgundy carpets and drapes were complemented by strategically placed live greenery.

The atmosphere exuded peace and efficient service as they entered. Paige would be inconspicuous, just another lodger—and Jonah was openly relieved by the presence of a young, observant doorman whose sharp eyes missed little.

There was also, the desk manager assured them, a security guard leased through a local agency. In his nine years at the front desk, not a breath of scandalous activity had smirched the good name of the hotel.

Jonah prayed it would stay that way.

As they waited for the elevator, Jonah's eyes roamed the foyer, analyzing, considering. One other couple entered the elevator when they did, and Jonah moved Paige into a corner, his body between her and the others. He relaxed only when they got off on the next floor, leaving Paige and Jonah to ride alone to the third floor.

"Jonah!" Paige finally broke the silence as they found her room and Jonah demanded the room key. "What are you doing?"

"We're not taking chances, Paige. Wait here in the hall until I can check the closets and bath."

When Jonah finally allowed her to enter the small, but

comfortable-looking room, she patiently promised that she still remembered Jay's unlisted phone number. "Jonah, I will call you—regardless of time—if I even *feel* uneasy."

"All right. I know you've had about all you can take," he reluctantly observed, regretting the brutal truths he had had to reveal. Her burned face and bruised forehead silently accused him.

"I'm fine," Paige promised, giving him a flickering smile that had all the light of a spent match.

You won't give up, will you, darling? "The hotel is fine. The weather is fine. You are not. Quit pretending—and don't argue," he added quietly when she opened her mouth. He moved over to the window and drew the drapes, then walked back to Paige. "Lie down—take a nap. I'm going back to the station and talk to the police, find out the latest on the professor's house."

"I want to—"

"Do as I suggest, right?" He met her defiant gaze calmly, unmoving. "Good. Lock the door. Don't open it unless you hear this sequence—" He rapped out a rhythm on the wall. "Paige?"

"All right."

Jonah frowned. She sat so still, hands clasped tightly together in her lap. The defiance had drained away, replaced by—what? He couldn't quite put his finger on it, but something wasn't right. "Well. . .I'll be going, then."

"Will you—" she bit her lip, shook her head. "All right," she repeated. "I'll see you later."

"Mm." He closed the door very quietly, waited until he heard her shoot home the dead bolt, then took the stairs instead of the elevator. Since the apartment was only two blocks away, he decided to trade Paige's car for his Harley. He could think on the Harley, and maybe between now and when he returned to Paige, he could figure out why she had metamorphosed from a valiantly coping woman to a lifeless automaton.

Was it the professor? The fire? Her apartment? His brush with the gunman?

Or was it something altogether different? He grimly promised himself that the mystery of Professor Kittridge's murder was not the only one he planned to solve.

CHAPTER 11

Paige spent a lot of time praying during the next twenty-four hours. Too numb to argue, she allowed Jonah to bully her nicely into staying at the hotel and plowing through scattered notes he retrieved from the mess at her apartment while he worked with the police, handling an endless, wearying hodge-podge of details concerning the fire.

Nothing was left of Professor Kittridge's house but rubble and ash. All his research, the files, the books—the legacy of a quarter-century—were gone. Paige was remotely grateful that the P.O.W. book was already in galley form. She had called the publisher, and they had promised to send an extra set within a week.

The professor's campus office had been sealed while the police conducted their investigation. Paige, however, would be allowed access as soon as she felt up to it.

She didn't feel up to it yet.

Moving stiffly, she wandered around the hotel room, her thoughts disjointed, a kaleidoscope of memories, feelings, theories, and—running through it all like spreading yeast—an undercurrent of fear. She scooped up her purse from one of the double dressers and tugged out a now crumpled envelope.

What if she hadn't left it in the car?

It was ironic, really. The information had been in her purse,

60

and she had left it on the seat. Professor K had been murdered, his house burned, Paige's apartment ransacked—and the clues were in her purse, lying forgotten in the car. Even Jonah hadn't noticed its presence until later.

If only they knew what they meant. A list of names. A key. A slip of paper with some more names.

If only shock and panic hadn't completely wiped from her memory the addresses she'd found the night of the fire.

Paige unfolded both lists, sinking down in a chair. Minton. Rand. Hoffelmeyer. . .her fingers clenched abruptly. Which names had caused such an exaggerated response from the professor? None of them matched the barely decipherable ones on the sheet of notebook paper he'd felt compelled to hide. What *was* the cryptic message scrawled within these papers that had caused someone to commit murder? *Why couldn't she remember what she'd dug out of Professor K's files?*

Three fast, two slow raps on the door startled her.

Paige opened it, coloring a little when Jonah smiled down at her. His hair was tousled, and his oxford cloth shirt clung in damp patches. No doubt he'd been running around on that wretched motorcycle he loved so much.

"Let's go down to the lobby," he murmured, swiping a hand across the perspiration dotting his face and forehead. "We need to make some plans."

Paige obediently gathered her purse and leather portfolio crammed with notes. Descending the elevator in silence, they chose an out-of-the-way corner in the almost deserted lobby. Jonah patted a damask rose-colored wingback chair opposite the sofa where he sat down. "Sit. Let's talk. Where're the lists of names?"

Paige held them out. His fingers brushed against hers, sending an unexpected jolt through her. Blinking, she slowly withdrew her hand, glancing at Jonah. He gave no sign that her touch had affected him in any way.

"I've decided," he said, looking at the lists, "that you're right. We don't have much choice but to have a go at finding out who these people are, track down addresses, maybe pay them a visit. It'll take longer now that we can't use the professor's files, but there's not much else to go on."

"We *might* pay a visit to a murderer."

"Mmm. At least we'd have a face to put with a name. Right now we're like a couple of toy ducks at a carnival."

"What did the police say?"

Jonah put his glasses on. "That it's my fool neck, and if I interfere with *their* investigation, they'll arrange to ship me off to my mother, among other things." Beneath the auburn moustache, his mouth kicked upward. "I had to tell them my alter ego—so now they not only know I'm J. Gregory, but that Mother is the British *grand dame* of archaeology."

Paige folded her hands in her lap. "I called my folks. My father wants me to fly home."

"So," Jonah returned very softly, "do I."

"Well, I'm not going to, so put your bag of British charm away. It won't work this time."

"You know me so well." He reached across and touched her hand. "Are you better today, Paige?"

"A little. I still have trouble talking about it. I feel like such a—a failure."

"Don't be ridiculous." He tilted his head, one broad fore-finger lifting to absentmindedly stroke his moustache. "You've got a fair-sized guilt complex for such an intelligent, attractive, eminently *professional* lady. I find that rather puzzling." He quit stroking the moustache and reached for the portfolio, his manner becoming brisk. "I'll be getting to the bottom of that, too—but not right now. We've work to do, Paige Elizabeth Hawthorne."

Paige stared at the milk glass basket of fresh flowers on the low table in front of them until her racing pulse slowed. "Who do we start with?" she managed to ask in an even voice. "The names on Professor K's list, or the ones on the World War II list?"

"Either—both." He hesitated, then spread his hands in a rueful gesture. "I know you'd prefer to go one way while I dig the other so we could accomplish twice as much with half the time—but I can't." He leaned forward, the deep blue eyes searching her face. "This is only going to get more dangerous. And like we discussed yesterday—we're pretty much on our own."

"I know." Paige shifted, then sat up straighter. "I'll be okay."

"I plan to try and insure that," Jonah said dryly. "But you *have* had a rather sheltered life, little *hana*. You might have scraped up the grit to brandish a butcher knife at me, but we both know you're not really equipped to cope with violence. Few sane people are."

"You being one of them." Her voice matched his for dryness.

"The streets I grew up on were a little more, um, rigorous than yours, yes."

Momentarily diverted, Paige found herself voicing questions she'd been too reserved to ask—until now. "You don't talk about your past much. I've been working with you for six months and don't know a whole lot beyond the blurb on all your cover jackets." She slanted him a sideways glance, "And that's pretty vague—not even a photograph."

Unconsciously, Paige stiffened, steeling herself for a rejection.

But Jonah surprised her this time, His reply was prompt and matter-of-fact, as if he knew she needed more from him now than his understated public persona.

"I had a rather. . .unusual childhood, probably largely due to a unique relationship with my parents." He shook his head.

"Two Oxford dons who make the professor's personality as bland as milquetoast." He smiled a smile full of nostalgia. "During the school year, I was at prep school with a lot of other snotty little boys who—as boys do—picked on the smallest, the odd man out, which always seemed to be me. I traveled with my mother in the summers. By the time I was twelve, I'd visited places all over the world that even my father couldn't pronounce."

"Is that why—" She stopped, not knowing how to phrase her question.

"Why I—write books? Settled in America? Drive you to distraction calling you names in an assortment of languages?" Starpoints of twinkling amusement lit up the night-dark eyes.

"Why you know how to take out a prowler and a man with a gun without batting an eye," Paige snapped in exasperation. "Why did you learn all that stuff?"

Jonah leaned forward, humor fading as he planted his elbows on his knees. "I got tired," he stated flatly, "of being picked on because I was undersized and wore glasses. Because I wouldn't conform to their image of the son of a professor *emeritus* of English and a famous mother. Children are cruel—and sometimes they never outgrow it." His hand shot out suddenly and swept Paige's hair back, tucking it behind her ear. "Did you get teased a lot about your ears? Is that why—even when you're half-dead from a fire—you try to make sure your hair covers them?"

Her face felt as hot as fire, and she jerked backward, her hands automatically flying up to prove Jonah's point. "I thought we were going to discuss the list of names, not my personal shortcomings."

"All right." He sat back, and Paige released a sigh of relief. "Let's get going, then. I imagine dropping in for a chat with your old chums at the Smithsonian might be a good place to start. You used to work at the Museum of American History, right?" He stood and pulled Paige to her feet. "At least we're both top-drawer researchers. We'll be able to keep our eyes skinned for necessary info as opposed to oddments that tend to trip one up."

"Thank you," Paige murmured quietly. Jonah paused from gathering up the lists, querying her with a lifted brow. Paige waved her hand, at a loss to explain. "For not treating me like—a—like I was—"

"You're welcome." He looked down at her a minute longer, a strange, intense expression growing in his eyes. Suddenly his head lowered.

It was a brief kiss, but so unexpected that Paige just stood there, unable to move. *Why had he done that?* Her mouth still felt the imprint of his, the surprising softness of his moustache. The sudden tenderness after months of a strictly maintained professional relationship threw her completely off guard. Her cheeks flamed.

Jonah's hand lifted to cup her heated face. "You're a top-drawer person in many ways, Paige Hawthorne." The hand slid beneath her hair, and his fingers traced the contours of her ear. "And that includes your ears. Now let's get started with our itinerary, and see about finding a dozen or so needles in acres of haystacks."

Three days later, they were at the professor's Georgetown office when Paige's contact at the Army Pentagon Library provided their first lead. But it was a name from the World War II list instead of the professor's.

"Minton, Gerald Payne. At least the initials match." Paige hung the phone up with satisfaction. "He served in the Diplomatic Corps—was stationed in England during the war. Permanent home address listed as Dayton, Ohio."

"Are you game for a lot of undoubtedly wasted travel time?"

"If it will help find whoever murdered the professor and tried to murder us, it's not wasted time."

Paige knew her voice sounded irritable. She wasn't surprised when Jonah crossed over to join her at the phone. She felt as highly strung as a cat trying to tiptoe through a yard full of pit bulls. Her eyes felt indelibly bloodshot; her nose was probably permanently wrinkled from hours and hours of searching through files, microfiche, the Smithsonian's SIBIS. . .even old court records.

And all the time, hovering at the edge of her consciousness crouched the chilling awareness that somewhere—maybe even in the same buildings they had visited—one or more men waited for the opportunity to kill them. The anonymous hotel merely provided a facade of security. Jonah might have picked up some evasive maneuvers over the years, but he was neither a trained agent, nor a detective. It was only a matter of time. . . .

The police had found the dark blue Nissan the gunman had used. It had been stolen from a computer programmer in Maryland and ditched at Dulles International Airport. There were no fingerprints other than smeared ones of the owner. Since Jonah had never had a clear view of the man's face, there was no way to ID him.

They needed a break. *She* needed a break.

"Paige?"

That was all. Just her name. She felt the bone-grinding tension crumble all of a sudden, leaving her quivering and vulnerable. Her head lifted, and she looked into eyes so darkly blue they were almost the polished black of a raven's wing.

"The Lord will keep both of us safe." He picked up her hand and held it. "And He'll provide peace, too, if you let Him."

"I know. It's the *not* knowing that is so hard to bear."

"Maybe Ohio will change that." He dropped her hand and picked up the phone.

CHAPTER 12

Gerald Payne Minton had died in 1980, but they located his son in Columbus. Patrick Payne Minton was a former city manager who was now a state senator in the Ohio General Assembly. After securing a late afternoon appointment, Jonah and Paige rented a car and drove from the airport to his office.

The honorable Mr. Minton was a gigantic bear of a man, well over six feet tall, with short-cropped ash-blond hair and wary brown eyes. He stayed seated behind his massive cherry desk, though he held his hand across to shake Paige's and Jonah's. He had a firm, no-nonsense grip, but one without any personal warmth.

"I understand you need information on my father," he announced without preamble after waving them to sit down. Glancing at his watch, he shuffled a few papers, then placed his hands flat on the desk. "I'm still a little unclear as to why."

Jonah relaxed back in the leather chair and looked at Paige. They had discovered some months earlier that Paige—particularly when dealing with men—was better at breaking the ice, disarming the people they interviewed with her genuine interest and lack of aggression.

"As I explained over the phone, I'm trying to complete a book written by Emil Kittridge," Paige began. "It compares

P.O.W.s in the various wars and is part of a multi-authored series under the auspices of the American History Association." She paused, waiting to see if there was any reaction. "The professor. . .died rather suddenly. . .and very recently, so I'm having to backtrack a few sources. Your father's name was on a list."

"My father spent the last fifteen years of his life in a nursing home," Minton said, his brown eyes as unrevealing as polished stones. "He suffered from Alzheimer's."

"I'm sorry." Paige gripped the pen she was holding more tightly. "I know that was painful."

Minton seemed to relax marginally. "Well, yes. It was. I'm afraid those years pretty much wiped out most of my memories of better times." He picked up an onyx letter opener, fiddled with it, then laid it back down. "You said you were particularly interested in his war experiences, but I'm not sure why. He was never a prisoner of war."

"He was in the Diplomatic Corps, wasn't he?" Jonah inserted, crossing his legs and contemplating the sole of his shoe. "In England?"

"I believe so. Look—I hate to be rude, but I've got another appointment in five minutes. I'm sorry you flew all the way out here for nothing, but I did warn you when you called from D.C. yesterday that I probably couldn't tell you anything."

"Is there a chance you might have some boxes of memorabilia—old letters, newspapers? Anything that might give us a clue?"

"There might be some stuff in the attic, but I don't know when I'll have time—" An intercom buzzed discreetly, and the secretary informed him that Mr. Larchant had arrived.

Minton stood. "Can you give me a month or so? Maybe when we're in recess over the holidays I can see if there's anything useful. World War II, right?"

"And anything after," Paige added. She looked at Jonah,

who rose lazily to his feet.

"You're running again next year?" he asked as Minton walked them to his door.

"That's the name of the game. I'd like to be able to spend more time with my constituents, of course, but anymore, raising funds for the campaign takes most of my time."

He extended his hand to open the door. "Thanks for stopping by. Sorry I couldn't be more help."

"What do you think?" Seated across from Jonah at a fast-food restaurant, Paige idly stirred an unwanted soft drink with her straw.

Jonah shrugged. "He was smooth but very evasive." He laughed wryly. "The perfect politician. I suppose it would have been much too pat to have everything fall together the first time. I don't even allow that in my books."

"He didn't want to talk about his father, did he?" She shoved the drink aside and leaned across to search Jonah's face. "Did you notice how he tensed up?"

"Mm. . .but it could have been because the memories are still uncomfortable. Be careful not to read more into—what is it?" Paige's eyes had widened suddenly, her mouth dropping open, then shutting. Jonah waited, unmoving, though his body hummed with alertness.

"There's a man standing in line—I think it's the same man I noticed when you were filling out the paperwork for the rental car at the airport."

She spoke quietly, but her hands fluttered like panicked birds. Jonah leaned forward until their noses were almost touching. "Describe him," he murmured. "No—don't back away from me. I want it to look like we're—um—oblivious to the rest of the world." He smiled. "Just look at me, my little *hatzvi*, and talk."

Exasperation shot across her face. "Someday, Jonah

Sterling...!" She flashed a brilliant, albeit artificial smile back. "He's wearing tan slacks—casual, not dress, striped shirt. Brown loafers. Sort of lanky, longish dark hair. He looks...uncomfortable." She bit her lip. "I'm not sure. I could be wrong. But if he followed us—he probably knows where we're staying in D.C."

Jonah's hand closed over hers. He lowered his voice. "Let's try a little experiment." He regarded her thoughtfully, and a glint flashed through the somber eyes. "Paige, I'm going to kiss you, so don't jump or pull away. Then I'm going to go order some fries or something. It'll be natural if you follow me with your eyes." He watched her reaction, the smile deepening. "But only if you look appropriately smitten instead of like a startled deer."

Without waiting for a response, he touched his mouth to hers, hearing her quick little intake of breath. Her lips trembled, then relaxed beneath his. "I'll go order some more," he said in a normal tone.

He sauntered up and joined the line of people, smiling at everyone in general as he pulled out his wallet. Two lines over, the dark-haired man shifted and turned. Jonah felt his skin tighten, teasing the base of his neck.

A few moments later he strolled back to Paige. The man was eating at a table with a good view of all the exits.

"We can eat this in the car." He clasped her wrist and urged Paige to her feet. "Our flight leaves in less than two hours."

"Why did you say that loud enough for him to hear?" Paige hissed the minute they were inside the car. Three cars down, the lanky man climbed into a black Camaro.

"To see his reaction." He glanced across at her, adding gently, "And because it's better to know than to walk in ignorance. Now I can see if he follows us and, if so, the kind of car he's driving."

"Jonah. . ."

He waited, dividing his attention between traffic and the black Camaro in the rearview mirror. They were five miles down the freeway before Paige spoke again.

"I'm sorry, Jonah, and I hate to admit it, but I'm scared."

The apologetic confession ripped through Jonah's insides like a grenade. He gripped the steering wheel tighter. "I know." He risked a quick survey of her rigidly upright body. "I am, too."

Her head snapped around. "*You're* scared?"

Her astonishment almost made him laugh. "I never deluded myself into thinking I was Superman after about the age of eight. I can defend myself, and I've had to a time or two in some tricky situations, but I was petrified every time." He watched the Camaro pass two cars and settle behind them again, four vehicles back. "Um. . .want to hear a story?"

"I'd like that, if you're sure you wouldn't mind."

"For you, I don't mind." The Camaro moved up another car. Jonah began weighing options while he tried to keep Paige distracted. "Remember I told you I used to spend summers with my mother? Well, I suppose it would have been more accurate to say that after she gave me the standard greeting upon my arrival, she'd be off to the dig, and I'd pretty much be on my own."

"That's terrible."

"Not really. When I was still a pint-sized boy, she'd hire a couple of locals to more or less watch out for me. One of them—when we were in the Hokkaido region of Japan—was a wiry little old man who'd been a master in the art of *ninjutsu.*"

He pressed the accelerator, speeding up a little. The Camaro closed the distance between them, pulling in directly behind them. The man driving lifted his hand—and drank from a large plastic cup. Jonah's shoulders relaxed infinitesimally as he resumed the autobiographical sketch.

"I was about nine or ten and an eager pupil. By the time I flew back to England, I was accomplished enough that the next time the school bully filched my glasses and wouldn't give them back, I made him.

"When I was fifteen, I spent a summer with Mother in Germany. I was too old to have a nanny—and by that time I was pretty much used to shifting for myself." He glanced across at Paige. "I joined a local gang and learned a rather nasty form of fighting. I rather enjoyed it, unfortunately, but I wasn't a Christian then."

"No wonder you take all this in stride. . . ."

"Not always. Paige, relax. I'm pretty sure the bloke in the Camaro isn't following us deliberately. He's much too obvious. And besides—he's eating."

Paige turned and looked over her shoulder while Jonah continued to monitor the rearview mirror. The man was indifferently chewing on a paper-wrapped burger now. They drove by an exit—and the Camaro disappeared down the ramp.

Jonah glanced across at Paige. "False alarm, huh? Can't say that bothers me." Surreptitiously, he wiped his palms, one at a time, on his slacks. "I guess we've started seeing villains behind every tree."

Paige's head drooped. She wouldn't look at him. "I'm sorry," she mumbled. "I'm being paranoid."

"Would you stop—" he gnawed furiously on the corner of his moustache a full minute before he was able to observe calmly, "Until we know what's going on, we're pretty much locked into a certain amount of paranoia. Try to keep a lid on that over-reactive guilt complex of yours, love."

He reached across the seat and playfully tugged her hair. "Smile for me," he commanded, "—or I'll call you something frivolous and frightfully obnoxious in, hmm —German, perhaps?"

Paige shook her head, but he could see her trying not to smile. Relieved, they drove the rest of the way in companionable silence, enjoying the brief respite from shadow dodging.

Jonah, however, silently wondered what might be waiting for them back in Washington.

"I told you not to call me—you were fired. Your ineptitude is inexcusable."

"Look, pal—maybe you need to realize you're not dealing with some scuzzbucket punk. So I missed a time or two. I got a handle on 'em now. If you'd provided a simple plane ticket, I could've had 'em. They've been out-of-town.

"You have been replaced." The freezing voice made his spine crawl.

"You can't do that!"

"I already have. You are a trigger-happy pyromaniac. I told you I needed those names. You failed to deliver the services for which I hired you. You'd be wise to watch your incompetent back, though I have my doubts as to your ability to accomplish even that."

Boiling with anger and fear the man slammed down the phone. "I'll show that armchair general," he muttered. "I'm gonna nail those two if it's the last thing I do. . . ."

CHAPTER 13

They took a taxi from the airport to Jonah's apartment. Paige waited in the cab while he dashed up the steps to drop off his hang-up bag and check the answering machine. When he returned a few minutes later, his expression was grim.

"What is it?" Paige asked, nervously twisting her head to see if the taxi had been followed.

Jonah stared out the window. "Later," he murmured, and Paige felt her skin grow cold.

At the hotel, he made her wait in the lobby until he checked her room out. Rejoining her in the lobby, he was silent as they rode the elevator up to her floor. Then he told her to pack up—she was leaving. Paige unlocked the door to her room, looked around the clean, innocent-looking space, then studied Jonah's impassive face. "All right," she said after a moment.

Thirty minutes later, after paying for her week's lodging, she and Jonah headed for their usual secluded corner of the lobby.

"What's happened?" She took a deep breath. "I've done what you asked without questioning because at the time it seemed prudent. But before I go another step, you're going to fill me in. Regardless of your opinion, I'm not made of cotton candy."

Jonah's gaze scanned the lobby, then returned to her face. "Jay's apartment got the same treatment as yours, so they've found where I've been living. That means they'll soon be able to trace you here. I can't figure out. . . ." His voice trailed away, and he shrugged. "At any rate, we're leaving before they find you."

"I—see." Paige's chin lifted. "How about the Castille? It's only a couple of blocks off the Mall, so it's fairly central to our research." She was proud of her even tone.

"It's expensive."

"It's safer than staying here." She worried the clasp of her purse. "You won't stay at the apartment now, will you?"

"No, little *Blume*. We'll both enjoy living in the lap of luxury for awhile, hmm. . . ."

"You do it on purpose, don't you?" She watched him, and the slow grin spreading across his face surprised her into relaxing the death clutch on her purse. "Whenever you think I'm too serious—or tense or—or frightened, you trot out one of those names."

He wrapped his hand about her elbow and ushered her toward the door. "Like I said, you know me very well."

They left The Bergman through a side entrance, and while Jonah watched, Paige called a cab from a pay phone. At the Castille, they were booked into adjoining rooms on the second floor. Instead of an elevator, they climbed a wide, "Gone With the Wind" staircase. Paige was too edgy to enjoy the ambience, particularly when Jonah prowled around the two rooms, searching corners with the relentless diligence of a trained German Shepherd sniffing out intruders.

Somehow, it wasn't reassuring.

Paige and Jonah spent a tedious, surprisingly non-threatening two days researching for information on both lists of names. Late in the afternoon of the second day, as they trudged past the front desk of the hotel, the clerk called them over, handing them two messages from a couple of their research contacts, and a large parcel.

"The galleys," Paige said, both excited and relieved. "Maybe now I can find some information on those names the professor went to such lengths to hide."

"Right-o," Jonah murmured, so absently Paige glanced up swiftly. He intercepted the look and handed her one of the messages.

Paige read it while they climbed the stairs to their rooms. "Interesting," she finally observed. "Right in our own back yard, and we didn't even know it."

"How many people know all five-hundred-odd names of Congressional members?"

Paige tossed him a quick look. "We'll have to give him a call and see how many secretaries and general dogsbodies we have to wade through."

"He's from Georgia."

"I see that," Paige returned, levity draining away. She stopped outside the door to her room and exchanged a long look with Jonah. "I'll start the calls; meet you for supper at seven."

The Honorable Armand Gladstone, Representative from the State of Georgia, arranged to meet them at the prestigious Domingo Club, a favorite haunt of members of Congress.

"He must be out to impress us, since we're not his constituents," Jonah observed in the taxi the next afternoon. "Lunch, plus an interview. . ."

"I've eaten there," Paige returned indifferently. "It's impressive only if you're impressed by that sort of thing."

"Ah well, at least we get a free lunch out of it."

Paige smiled; when the cab dropped them off, she couldn't help checking to make sure her hair was arranged and her linen suit was straight, wrinkle-free. When she caught Jonah's surprisingly tender look, she colored, then marched up the marble steps into the Domingo.

A tall, well-built man with imposing brows, huge beaked nose and impeccably styled silver-black hair, Congressman Gladstone welcomed them with a polished smile and outstretched hand. The garnet from a signet ring glittered in the subdued lighting of the foyer. It was so reminiscent of the meeting with Patrick Minton, Paige's answering smile almost broadened into laughter.

"Glad you could make it. I hope you don't mind, but I took the liberty of ordering ahead." He waved them toward the dining room. "I'm pretty pushed for time."

"We're familiar with the complaint," Jonah concurred, his face bland. Paige made a face at him behind the congressman's back.

Over shrimp cocktails, Gladstone shared his Vietnam experiences and how much winning the Bronze Medal had meant to him. He admitted that it had probably helped him win his congressional seat orginally, but hoped—with a deprecating smile—that his subsequent victories had been due to merit.

Over Boneless Breast of Chicken Bagatelle that looked better than it tasted, he and Jonah exchanged reminiscences about their respective childhoods. Armand's father had been in the Diplomatic Corps, and Armand was almost as well-traveled as Jonah.

"Did your father ever meet a man named Gerald Minton?" Paige inserted in a rare moment of silence.

Gladstone turned politely toward her. "The name isn't familiar," he admitted after a minute. He smiled. "But then in this position I meet so many people. . . ."

"What about your father?" Jonah casually reached over and speared the circular spiced apple Paige had shoved to one side of her plate. "Is he still alive? He might be more likely to know."

"Regretfully, though still alive, my father's health is so poor I'm afraid he wouldn't have much to offer. You say the book series is funded by a grant from the American History Association? I wonder I haven't heard of it."

"I would have thought," Paige ventured, her hands knotting in her lap while she kept her face serene, "that Professor Kittridge might have interviewed you at some point in the past couple of years. Even though you're not a former P.O.W., you are a Vietnam veteran."

The puzzled frown on the congressman's face cleared. "Oh—*that* book. The name didn't register the first time. As a matter of fact, we did have a talk some months ago, though for a different matter. It was some university function, I believe. He's pretty much of a character, isn't he? You should have brought him along. I would have enjoyed chatting with him again."

In the awkward ensuing silence, a discreet waiter removed their plates. "I'm afraid Professor Kittridge was—I'm afraid he died back in August." Paige twisted her hands under the table and almost jerked when she felt the warmth of a man's hand covering hers.

"It was sudden," Jonah explained, "which is why Mrs. Hawthorne is having to retrace some of his sources so she can proof the galleys. I'm—um—trying to help."

"The professor died?" The icy gray eyes softened. "I am sorry to hear that. I'm sure it's a great loss to the academic community."

They ate their raspberry flan in congenial silence, but the minute the waiter whisked the dishes away, Armand rose. "I have a committee meeting, so I'm afraid I must excuse myself." He gestured to a discreet young man who had miraculously appeared behind them. "Dennis will try to answer any further questions, and if you'd care for a tour of—"

"That won't be necessary." Jonah rose and held Paige's

chair. "Thanks for your time. We'll make sure you receive a complimentary copy of the professor's book."

The congressman paused. He turned back, staring down at Paige a minute. "Ah yes. It's nice to have someone so lovely and obviously conscientious who can step in and see that all his work is not in vain."

Jonah didn't change expression, or even move, but Paige gently insinuated herself between him and Armand. After thanking the congressman one final time, they left. Only when they were back in the taxi and moving did she release her pent-up breath.

"He was just playing his role, Jonah, And with even a little more warmth than Minton, I thought."

The midnight gaze rested on her a minute, and Paige felt an absurd desire to drop the matter, so she lifted her chin and faced him with cool control. "Do you think either of them could be involved? I thought it interesting that both their fathers were in the Diplomatic Corps—and now they're both in politics. Maybe that's the key to those nine names."

"I don't know." His hand lifted and his finger tucked her hair behind her ear.

Mesmerized by the gentle touch and the look still lingering in his eyes, Paige couldn't lift her hand to pull her hair back over her ear. "What's the matter? Why are you looking like that? Did I say something wrong? I'm sorry—" Even her vocal chords strummed with reaction to Jonah's bizarre behavior.

"I didn't like the way Gladstone treated you—looked at you," the mild-mannered Jonah Sterling replied calmly. "He's lucky I'm such a peaceable bloke. If he'd patronized you with one more silver-tongued remark, I might have been tempted to remove it for him."

Paige stared silently out the window until the taxi stopped in front of their hotel. Who *was* this man?

CHAPTER 14

Just before closing time late Thursday afternoon in the Modern Military Headquarters Branch of the National Archives, Paige found another name of the "Pettigrew," list as they'd dubbed the nine names.

"Brewster Covington, charged with embezzling government payroll. Sentenced to five years. Dishonorable discharge," Paige read aloud, excitement skimming through her exhaustion. "This happened in '48, after the war, but the initials fit . . . ."

Jonah dropped the paper airplane he'd been constructing out of scrap paper. Scooting his chair from his study carrell to Paige's, he twitched the publication around. "Let's go for it," he said after a minute. "If we hurry, we might have an address in time to catch a flight tomorrow afternoon, if it's impractical to drive."

Last known address for Brewster Covington was Hamlet, Missouri. A garrulous operator connected them to a friend of a friend of a second cousin who used to live next door to Covington's grandmother. Paige watched Jonah's low-key, amalgamated blend of Oxford English and Tidewater drawl work its charm. Every now and then he'd cut his eyes to Paige, bathing her in the warmth of his slow smile.

They finally learned that Brewster had settled in California sometime in the 'fifties. By the following afternoon, they had an address and reservations on a red-eye flight leaving Dulles a little after eleven that night.

They drove Paige's car to the airport, but due to extensive construction, they had to park in a satellite parking lot a mile or away. Paige dozed most of the way to the airport and was still in a stupor as Jonah drove slowly up and down the poorly lit rows of cars, searching for a vacant spot.

He turned another corner—and inhaled sharply, hitting the brake with enough force to jerk Paige fully awake. "Jonah?"

"I'm afraid we may have trouble."

She watched him glance around. They were several hundred yards away from the ticket booth, and, at this time of night, there were few other signs of life.

"What is it?"

"There's a car that's been following us, staying exactly four cars behind, since two blocks from the Castille. And, I saw the figure of a man just now, when I turned down the aisle, that was too suspiciously familiar for my peace of mind."

He hesitated, then released the brake so the car began slowly moving again. He switched on the bright headbeams. "Slide down in the seat," he instructed Paige. "You won't be as much of a target that way."

"What about you?"

"Pray," he shot back tersely. "There's a shuttle bus that ferries people to the terminal. I don't know how often it runs this time of night. Let's hope. . ." his voice trailed away as he pulled into a vacant parking space and killed the engine.

Paige tried to swallow, failed. "Where is he now?"

"He parked his car two aisles over. I saw him when he got out, but he's disappeared." He rapped the steering wheel, frowning.

The makeshift parking lot with its sparsely placed lights turned the area into a deathtrap. Paige could barely even see Jonah beyond an unmoving profile. She peered out into the darkness, searching, her heart thumping against her ribs.

Headlights suddenly bathed them in a yellow wash. A car was coming down their aisle. It parked several spaces down, and two men in business suits emerged. The air suddenly filled with raw electricity; Jonah's eerie stillness was almost as frightening as the man lurking somewhere in the shadows. Slowly, silently Jonah eased the window down a crack.

The two men from the car approached, their voices easily carrying in the night. Jonah's hand snaked out and pressed Paige's shoulder, keeping her still.

"...And then he said if we couldn't have it first thing in the morning, we'd lose the sale. . . ."

"Harry's always been a pain. . . ." The voices faded as the men walked hurriedly by, apparently hoping to catch the shuttle bus sooner, rather than waiting in the car.

"Come on." Jonah opened his door at the same time Paige opened hers. They caught up with the two men just as the shuttle bus entered the lot, a good quarter of a mile away.

Paige forced a smile for the men. They barely nodded before resuming their gripe session about flying to L.A. on short notice. Beside her, Jonah's body hummed with tension; his head swiveled constantly as he surreptitiously searched the long rows of cars shrouded in tomb-like silence.

The chugging of the bus and grinding gears drew closer.

Paige wiped her damp palms on her skirt, clutching the briefcase as if it were an armored vest. Would he shoot in front of witnesses? Would he just kill them, too?

The bus turned down the aisle next to them. Overhead, a departing plane filled the night with roaring noise, muffling out the sound of the bus—and anything else.

Jonah casually took Paige's arm and moved them out from

under the light, where they'd been waiting with the two men, and in between two parked cars. Paige felt the strength of his grip and knew with a flash of numb certainty that he was steeling himself to hurl her to the pavement.

The bus approached, blinding them in the glare of its headbeams. The two businessmen shifted impatiently. With a crunch of gears and a soft hissing as the doors opened, the bus lumbered to a stop. A shadow moved in the next aisle. Practically yanking her shoulder out of its socket, Jonah reached the open bus door in four long strides, shoving her up the steps if front of the businessmen.

On the painfully slow return trip to the terminal, Paige sat tensely on a seat across from the two businessmen, braced for the unknown. Waiting.

As the bus left the parking lot and turned onto the road to the airport, Paige twisted in the seat and saw a dark shape weaving an angry path down the aisles. She nudged Jonah.

"I see it," he said. His hand, resting on his knee, closed into a fist.

The bus rounded a curve; the parking lot, and the car, disappeared. The rest of the way to the terminal, Paige and Jonah listened half-heartedly to the businessmen's running litany of complaints on everything from the stock market to the inconvenience of catching a shuttle bus instead of being able to park near the terminal.

Jonah's head turned slightly to Paige. In the dim reflection of the interior lights, she caught the barely visible movement as a corner of his moustache lifted.

"I really am getting tired of this," Paige said shakily. Their flight had just been called, and they were waiting in line with a straggling crowd. Jonah took the briefcase from her betrayingly damp hands and tried to produce an encouraging smile.

To Paige, it looked more like a savage baring of teeth as his eyes surveyed the crowd around them. She felt his tension, but he didn't take it out on her. She swallowed around a sudden lump and rested her hand on his forearm. "We'll be okay," she promised softly, knowing that it might not be true. Right now, she didn't care. Right now all that mattered was easing Jonah's pain—like he had tried to soothe hers.

Even as she voiced the words, she was filled with a strange sense of peace. She smiled up at him, a surprised, then serene, heartfelt smile. "I do feel safe with you, even in the valley of the shadow of death."

Jonah's hand covered hers and squeezed. She felt him relax just a little.

Brewster Covington lived alone in a small house on the edge of the Mojave Desert in southern California. A thin layer of dust coated everything—even, it seemed—the gaunt, gray-haired Brewster Covington. In the unforgiving light of the morning sun it was plain that the years had not been kind. Cold eyes, narrowed with suspicion, appraised Paige and Jonah from behind the screen door.

"We tried to call," Paige wet her lips, attempting to smile coaxingly, "but your answering machine—"

"I heard it." He abruptly flung open the door. "Come in. Ya got five minutes."

Brewster volunteered a bucketful of information about his successful son's successful law practice—but no amount of coaxing succeeded in persuading him to share his war time experiences, much less the crime that put him in prison and ended his military career.

"The war's a dead issue—nobody cares anymore, including me. You want to hear about my son, I talk. Keep pestering me about a book I care nothin' 'bout—and you can just shag yourselves right outa here."

Six minutes later they were on the way to San Bernardino where Brewster Covington's son had established a law practice.

"He might see ya. He might not. Pretty busy man, my son. He's gonna be a judge, if he plays his cards right."

"Have you noticed," Paige commented while they ate lunch in a park near James Covington's firm, "that everyone connected with that list is in some kind of politics? And that nobody wants to talk about the war, even though it's been over for almost fifty years?"

"I noticed." Jonah tossed a piece of bread to a hopeful squirrel. "I'm beginning to think that whatever that list of names represents must be awful."

"I didn't think, when we found it behind the ribbons bar, that it was merely a list of people to invite to a tea party."

They finished lunch in silence, and an hour later a perfectly groomed and coifed secretary admitted them to James Covington's office. He immediately walked around his desk to meet them. The secretary brought in a silver tea service with coffee and an assortment of pastries.

"It was thoughtful of you to stop by—I don't get out to Dad nearly like I should." He sat down across from Paige and Jonah and helped himself to a confection. "Life's pretty hectic around here, and Dad. . .well, you might have gathered he's not the most sociable creature."

"Only when it comes to telling us about you," Jonah offered, his voice dry but devoid of mockery.

"We really needed to hear about his World War II experiences," Paige said. "I realize it was a long time ago, but—"

"With the situation what it is in Germany, and most of Europe, somehow World War II seems a little more relevant than it did a year ago." Covington smiled at her, and from the corner of her eye Paige saw—no, *felt*, Jonah shift uneasily, the tension transmitting itself to her in inexplicable but disturbing waves.

They chatted with the lawyer for almost half an hour—and

found out nothing. He was married, had three children and a successful practice; he was planning to run for a judgeship in the elections next year. But throughout his life, his father and mother had steadfastly refused to discuss the war. In the end, Jonah rose with deceptive laziness, held out a hand to Paige, and thanked Covington for seeing them.

Nobody followed them to the L.A. airport, but the feeling of incipient despair continued to darken and swell. Paige knew they were lost in a maze of cryptic clues, and with every step, the walls closed in behind them.

CHAPTER 15

October settled over the city with warm Indian summer days and pleasantly cooler nights. Three days of drenching rain left Jonah and Paige with claustrophobia along with beleaguered spirits, so on the first clear day they escaped for a ride through the Virginia countryside—on the back of Jonah's Harley-Davidson motorcycle.

Paige hadn't protested too strenuously, in spite of the fact that Jonah had only been able to persuade her to ride behind him on the Harley on two other occasions.

They headed west on Highway 50, then turned onto Route 15; choking traffic, buildings, crowds, and noise gradually dwindled until they were replaced by hardwood forests, rolling hills, sprawling farms, and white fences. Brilliant red maples splashed the countryside with bright dollops of color, and Paige finally relaxed. She'd grown up riding horses on her father's farm—mostly bareback. This wasn't really so very different.

And she knew, on a deep subconscious level she refused to examine, that she *could* trust Jonah with her life. It had been years since she felt that way about anyone, and the realization was both exhilarating—and terrifying.

The wind roared past, blending with the muted roar of the Harley; after awhile Paige gave in and closed her eyes, allowing the pulsing noise and sensation of speed to lull her battered senses.

She had no warning when the peaceful October day shattered.

The Harley downshifted so suddenly Paige's head jerked up even as she instinctively tightened her grip on his waist. They whipped onto a small dirt road bisecting the state forest. Jonah flung out one booted foot to keep the bike from keeling over as they rounded a corner at a high speed. The muscles in his back and shoulders bunched, flowing with astonishing strength as he wrestled with the handlebars of the heavy machine.

Paige slipped sideways, grappling desperately for a handhold that wouldn't distract Jonah, and gripped the bike with her legs as if she were trying to stay on the back of a rearing bronc. Then Jonah recovered control, and the Harley shot down the winding road like a bullet fired from a gun.

Paige knew there was only one reason Jonah would be handling his prized Harley-Davidson in such a blatantly reckless manner. Suddenly, escaping from the suffocating hotel room and tomb-like research facilities didn't seem like such a good idea.

Something whined past Paige's head, sharp and stinging. She cringed, burrowing her helmet into the back of Jonah's leather jacket, then felt more than heard a muffled thunk in the vicinity of her left foot. Jonah abruptly turned the bike again, directly into the woods.

Paige risked turning her head. Fifty yards behind them, a blue car skidded to a halt. The Harley bounced, swerved drunkenly around a dense thicket of low-lying bushes, then wove a laboring, erratic path between pine, oak, and hickory trees.

Paige tried to keep her body limber enough to move with the twists and turns, but she felt more like a slab of concrete. When Jonah whipped the bike in a tight half-circle and stopped, skidding almost soundlessly on the pine-needle forest floor, she would have toppled over if his arm hadn't shot out and grabbed her.

He killed the engine, and deathly silence descended.

Paige carefully removed her helmet, her gaze focused toward the dirt road. Jonah had done the same. Unmoving, poised like some wild stag scenting the hunter, he surveyed the woods, watching, listening.

"There." Paige grabbed his shoulder, urgently pointing just as a bullet exploded in a white pine two feet away.

"Hold on!" Jonah crammed his helmet back on his head. The motor snarled into life. He plunged down a shallow slope, fought through a tangle of dying catbriar, and gunned the Harley up the other side of the slope, into even thicker woods.

He slowed down, maneuvering around rotting logs as well as trees and shrubs. Blackened trunks showed the ravages of a forest fire many years earlier.

Paige tried to keep from clinging, tried to keep her head high and alert toward the rear, where Jonah couldn't see. But her vision was obscured by her helmet; her fingers were numb, slippery. She kept losing her grip. *I'm sorry*, she told him silently, guilt and humiliation joining the terror. *I'm sorry*.

Time blurred into a jumbled sensation of sound and motion, and with every heartbeat, Paige waited for a bullet to slam into her vulnerable back.

They stopped and silence filled the forest.

Jonah's hands closed over hers and very gently eased them away from their desperate grip about his waist. He swung off the Harley and lifted Paige off. "Paige?" Just as gently, he eased the helmet off her head.

She looked up into his face, then slowly turned, her eyes searching the woods. "Where are they?"

"I'm pretty sure they didn't follow on foot too long, so I

89

imagine they're either trying to figure out where we'll surface—or they've gone back to the hotel to wait for us." He lifted her chin. "Buck up—we'll make it out okay."

Paige pulled free, took two wobbly steps and collapsed beneath a blazing yellow tulip tree. Breathing in uneven, shallow gasps, she stared fixedly at her knees until a wave of dizziness subsided. "What a lovely way to spend an afternoon," she mumbled.

Jonah's hand came down briefly on her shoulder, then lifted. "Wait here. I'm going to scout around a bit." He disappeared in the woods, so swiftly and silently a wave of fresh goosebumps rippled over Paige's skin.

What kind of man is he, really?

All the past months of working with him had not prepared her for such a shocking metamorphosis. Like. . . like Clark Kent to Superman. Like absentminded professor to Indiana Jones. Like—

She stood, clutching her elbows, concentrating fiercely on the vivid red berries in a tangle of bushes to keep from bursting into hysterical laughter.

When Jonah returned, he saw at a glance that Paige had been crying, though her face now was the picture of serenity, her smile almost natural. *Father, I love this woman. Help me keep her safe. . .please, Lord.*

"No sign of anything but deer—I saw some tracks." He dropped down beside her, picking up a leaf and tracing his finger over the intricate play of veins. "All quiet on the home front?"

"Like a tomb." She made a jerky motion with her hand. "Maybe I should use a different simile. . . ."

"I promised to keep you safe—" he looked at her until she dropped her gaze, "—and I will."

"Even the talented and literate J. Gregory—or the mighty

Jonah Sterling—is incapable of dodging bullets forever." She stood. "There's a hole in the rear fender of your Harley."

"What!" He leaped up and strode over to examine the damaged fender. "The insufferable twit!" he muttered, turning back to Paige and giving her a lopsided grin. "Now that's going too far, don't you think? It's one thing to take potshots at us, but when you get my Harley instead. . . ."

Paige was shaking her head, a glimmer of light spilling at last into the terror-darkened gray eyes. She crammed her fist against her mouth, but the amusement escaped anyway. Jonah walked back over.

"You never have exhibited proper respect for my machine," he complained, secretly delighted that his diversionary attempt had succeeded. He *was* angry about the damage to his bike, of course, but next to Paige, the Harley was just scrap metal.

That thought gave him a momentary pause. Then he saw tears slipping out the corners of her eyes and felt as if he'd taken a bullet in his heart. "Paige. . .love—don't. . . ." He put a hand on her arm, halting her when she would have backed away.

"I'm fine, fine." Her hands tried to push him aside. "You're just so f-funny about the Harley."

"Be still, woman, and let me hold you!" Jonah all but roared, yanking her right up against his chest and clamping his arms around her. "You don't have to be perfect, Paige. Do you hear me? You don't have to be perfect."

She suffered the embrace for a few minutes, but she stayed rigid, hands clenched in tight-fisted balls at her sides. Reluctantly, Jonah freed her, dropping his arms and stepping back as he fought to subdue his own wildly swinging emotions.

"I know I'm not perfect," Paige ground out, "and you don't have to baby me." She wiped the back of her hand over her eyes, looking impossibly disheveled and woebegone.

Jonah dropped down under the tree and patted the ground

91

beside him. "Come on—sit down by me." He waited until Paige slowly obeyed. Picking up another leaf, he twirled it idly round, his eyes watching the motion. "Do you think," he mused aloud after several moments, "that I'll think less of you if you don't handle yourself like Joan of Arc waiting for the torch?" Tossing the leaf aside, he tilted his head and peered down toward Paige's averted face. "It's not childish to want to be comforted after a scare—it's basic human need. Why won't you let me give you that?" He smiled a little. "I was scared, too. Maybe *I* need a hug as much as you. . . ."

Paige shrugged. Jonah waited, saying nothing. "At least you didn't act like a spineless wimp," she finally confessed bitterly. "Ever since Professor K was murdered, that's all I've done." Her eyes darted upward, then away. "It's humiliating. I didn't use to be like that." She stopped.

"I see," Jonah said. He eased himself to a comfortable reclining position, arms draped behind his head, eyes closed. "What did you used to be like?" he asked comfortably, as if he'd asked her views on the preacher's sermon at the last church service.

He could feel her wariness, practically hear the bars clanging shut in the corridors of her mind. But much to his relief, after a minute she sighed and answered simply enough, "When I was a child, I was always the one my sisters could talk into trying something really dangerous — like jumping out of the hay loft, or cutting across the neighbor's field without letting his Angus bull see us. Standing on the back of one of my grandfather's horses at a full gallop. Nothing nearly as exciting as you—but at least I wasn't a coward."

"You're not a coward now."

"If you hadn't held on to me back there, I would have fallen, I was so terrified."

Jonah sat up. "I believe," he stated calmly, "that we've already covered this ground. Why is it so important for you not to admit any weakness? In all the months we've worked together, you've gone to torturous lengths to avoid any shows of vulnerability—until one morning when you walked into a situation over your head."

"Don't remind me," Paige muttered, streaks of red climbing up her cheeks.

"But I like the memory. You let me hold you, for the first time." He drew the leaf down her arm in a light, teasing path. "And I enjoyed that feeling very much."

"Hadn't we better be leaving?"

Jonah laughed. "Not yet, little *Schildkrote*. I want to recover my breath first and continue this very interesting conversation."

Paige grabbed a handful of leaves and soil and tossed it at him, the laughter back in her eyes. "How many languages do you know, anyway?" she asked in exasperation.

He grinned. "A working knowledge of four or five. I always picked up the dialect of whatever country I spent the summer with Mother in. For some reason God gave me an ear for languages. It used to infuriate Mother, who couldn't even manage a simple "thank you" without a two-language dictionary." He absently brushed the dirt and leaves off his jacket and jeans, lost in a haze of memories.

"Why don't you ever go on promo tours as J. Gregory?" Paige asked out of the blue, startling Jonah so much he was momentarily at a loss.

"I—um—I detest the circus atmosphere—being so mercilessly exposed to the public eye." He shook his head. "What on earth made you ask something like *that*?"

The color in her cheeks deepened. "You have to know you're a fascinating, intriguing man. I've been around highly educated people ever since I was a freshman at Georgetown, but I never met anyone who could speak three languages, much less four or five. Or who'd been all the places and experienced what you have. You'd probably sell twice as many books."

"I want people to read my books for the story—and the Christian message—not as a sop to my ego," Jonah murmured. He felt awkward but elated by Paige's observation—and with an urgent need to explain. "The few times I agreed to speaking engagements, nobody saw, well—me. They saw their own idea of J. Gregory, author, adventurer. . .'super-Christian'." He looked away from Paige, feeling even more embarrassed. "It was awful. I feel, you know, that God gave me whatever talent and success I've enjoyed to further *His* kingdom—not the popularity of a man called J. Gregory."

He finally looked back over at Paige, who was staring at him with a peculiar, arresting expression on her face. "Do you understand?" he asked, feeling diffident, almost sheepish. Why was she staring at him like that?

"I understand."

He heaved a sigh of relief and grinned at her. "Thanks, love. That's why having such an exemplary—not to mention discreet—assistant proves invaluable. Paige? What are you thinking?"

"I'm wondering—" Paige hesitated, tugging a lock of hair and wrinkling her nose before finishing in a rush, "I'm wondering how you stay so—*sane* is the word that comes to my mind—beneath the pressure of constantly having to produce a best-seller that's better than the one before. Do you ever want to just chuck it all? Do you—oh, never mind. This is ridiculous."

She started to rise, and Jonah reached up an arm, tugging her back down. "I write the books," he said. "It's not up to me how well they sell, if they sell at all. It's up to God." He scrutinized her face more closely, and it was almost as if a curtain lifted. "Was that how you used to feel? That you were always on center stage, expected to perform in a superlative manner—

or you were a failure?"

She flushed to her hairline. "The parallel did occur to me, even though I know it's presumptuous to compare my life to yours."

Jonah twisted to a kneeling position directly in front of her so rapidly Paige flinched. His hands closed over her elbows. "Don't ever let me hear you say something like that again." He heard the clipped words with an inward groan. *This woman can really irritate me, Lord. But you knew that already, didn't you? Thanks.* "You're responsible to God, just as I am. You don't have to live up to my standards—or your friends'—not even your church. Paige, you know better than that."

"I used to think so." She squirmed, trying to free herself. "Can we go now? It's going to be dark in a few—"

"Right." He dropped her arms and stood. "In case you were wondering—*Schildkrote* is 'turtle' in German, and that's exactly what you remind me of right now, when you're so uncomfortable with a conversation all you want to do is hide in your shell."

He strode back over to the Harley and, without a word, secured the helmets to the bars, then turned the machine back east. "Let's go, then."

CHAPTER 16

He'd never shown impatience or anger at her before, Paige reflected, torn between swelling hurt, and confusion. In fact, less than a week ago she'd relished the warmth of his understanding support. It must be her fault. It *was* her fault.

As she walked over to him, she made the painful decision just to let the matter drop. Like she had always done. Like a turtle in its shell. *Yep, that's what you are, Paige. First a coward—and now a turtle. At least it answers the question of what Jonah thinks of you, doesn't it?*

She lifted her chin, squaring her shoulders and gathering her reserve. Jonah was ready to leave, and she didn't need to keep him waiting.

"I'd like to apologize."

Nonplussed, Paige stopped in her tracks and stared. "What?"

He was dragging his leather gloves through his hand, slapping them in his palm, and though he still looked impatient—he also looked contrite. "I know it upsets you when I don't control my temper. We're both off balance, scared—I shouldn't have bullied you."

Paige stood in front of him, struggling to search behind the wooden mask of his face. *What temper?* "You didn't bully me." She swallowed, steeling herself to admit candidly, "You were right, at any rate."

"Mmph." His mouth beneath the moustache twitched. "In

that case, let's kiss and make up, so we can find our way out of these woods." The gloves dropped down on the top of his helmet. "Come here."

Paige backed a step. "I don't think so."

Jonah stepped around the Harley. "But I do. Don't retreat into your shell, little *Schildkrote*. . . ."

Paige backed another step. "Why are you acting like this? We could be shot dead any minute—this is very adolescent of you. . .Jonah—" She bumped into a tree.

He trapped her there by planting his hands on the trunk on either side of her head. "You're absolutely delectable when you're flustered," he teased with exaggerated British pompousness. Then he leaned forward, dropped a brief kiss on her protesting lips, and stepped back. "There—an apology and a reward all at once."

Paige touched her fingers to her lips. She still felt the warm, firm pressure of Jonah's lips. "I thought you were irritated . . . ."

"I got over it. I'm not a monster, Paige—and I'm not an adolescent, either." He lifted her hand. "What I am is a man who—" His eyes narrowed to black diamond slits as his gaze slowly traversed Paige from head to foot. "I begin to see. . ." he murmured.

Paige watched in bewilderment as he kissed the back of her hand, then placed it in the crook of his arm. He led her back over to the Harley without saying another word.

"What do you see?" she had to ask when it was obvious he wasn't going to elaborate on his oblique statement.

Jonah had pulled on his gloves and was scanning the surrounding woods. "I see," he said without looking at her, "a lot more every day." He glanced over his shoulder. "There'll be a certain amount of—um—risk, maneuvering my bike through these woods, but I think the risk outweighs the greater danger of being trounced on by a gunman if we go back the way we came."

He really could be a *very* exasperating man, Paige decided with rueful resignation. "What if they hear the motor and follow the sound?" she asked, determined to adopt the same nonchalant pose, regardless of her churning insides.

"I'm pushing the bike. We'll be walking. Think you can make it, Little Red Riding Hood?" His gaze swept over her again, from untidy hair to serviceable leather ankle boots.

"I can make it."

The warm approval in his eyes gave Paige a funny, almost choking sensation in her chest. She hadn't realized until now how much she coveted being the recipient of that look—until it had been absent. She covered the rush of emotion by flashing a bright smile. "Maybe Grandma's at the other end with cookies and milk, since the wolves are hopefully engaged elsewhere."

"That's my—"

"*Don't* say it!"

In the deepening twilight they grinned at each other—and Paige felt, at last, that their relationship rested on solid ground again.

Then Jonah's hand lifted to move, featherlight across her cheek."You're doing fine, Paige," he said softly, seriously. "Nobody could have behaved better."

"I'm still scared."

"That's okay—so am I."

She walked beside Jonah almost an hour, struggling with both the gnawing fear and her growing awareness of him. Every now and then she glanced across, unwillingly admiring the supple strength of his deceptively lean body. Admiring, as well, his attitude.

The Harley was heavy, a dead weight, but Jonah didn't complain. He was covered with perspiration, even though the afternoon had cooled into the fifties, and he gratefully accepted Paige's help when they climbed yet another slope. But he didn't complain; he didn't blame Paige and tell her it was all her fault; he didn't bemoan the uncertainty of their situation. He smiled at her.

What kind of man *was* this? The more she learned about him, the less she knew. And the more she wanted to know.

The sunset faded to mauve and whitewashed blue. Eyeing the sky, then the endless forest with growing concern, Jonah called a halt. Paige collapsed by a sun-warmed boulder and leaned forward to loosen her boot laces.

"It doesn't look too good, does it?" she asked quietly.

"Mm. How about if you rest a bit, keep an eye on the Harley, and I'll do some more scouting around."

Paige immediately rose. "Why don't you let me do the scouting? I haven't been pushing that ugly monster the last hour or so." She steeled herself for flat rejection, maybe even another display of coolly controlled irritation. No. . .more probably it would be a masculine negative couched in humor, since Jonah wasn't venal. She'd always known that. . . .

"All right. I could use a rest."

Paige froze, gaping at him. He had pulled out a handkerchief and was wiping his face and brow, but his eyes held hers in a steady gaze. "Just don't get lost. I haven't the energy to track you down."

"I won't," Paige promised, clearing her throat. "I won't, Jonah." She looked around, establishing bearings and landmarks, making a note of the immediate surroundings. There seemed to be a lightness toward the southeast, possibly a break in the woods, so she headed off in that direction.

In spite of fear, fatigue, and aching feet, she suddenly wanted to laugh. He hadn't put her down. He'd treated her like an equal. Well, not precisely an equal. . .but like a person. Like a competent woman.

Lifting her head toward the sky, she hugged herself with

secret delight. Then she started scouting terrain.

A scant ten minutes later she found an abandoned hunting shack with a barely discernible track leading north. After returning to share the discovery with Jonah, they discussed options and finally agreed to risk riding the Harley. It was five-thirty, almost dark, and neither of them wanted to spend the night in a ramshackle cabin.

The track led to a dirt road, which cut southeast and brought them—unscathed—back to the highway. Jonah revved the bike, and they made it to McLean without incident.

"I'm sorry." Jonah regarded her unsmilingly as they ate supper before taking a roundabout route back to the hotel. "It was irresponsible of me to—"

"You sound like me. Stop it." Paige pointed her fork at him. "You know what I've finally accepted? We don't have much choice but to keep searching for clues, exposing ourselves, and praying for a break—'cause I don't think stopping now would alter our situation." She took a bite of her hamburger and chewed vigorously. "I have an idea."

Jonah groaned.

Paige ignored him. "Why don't we try talking to the person who donated Major Pettigrew's uniform? I know the lady—his daughter?—isn't trying to kill us, and maybe she'll have some more memorabilia, snippets of conversation she heard as a child."

"Maybe she *is* behind it all. Who knows?" Jonah pinched the bridge of his nose. "Everyone else we've talked to seems to have skeletons rattling or shaky motives to keep our suspicions lurching around in the dark. Why not her? Maybe she's a secret member of a society that detests college professors."

Paige grinned at his nonsense but stood her ground. "Well, have you got a better idea? Other than setting ourselves up as targets like we did this afternoon?" She regretted the words the minute they left her mouth, especially when Jonah flushed, and a veil seemed to blur the brightness of his gaze. "Jonah, I'm sorry."

She reached out a hand in a gesture of apology and knocked his drink into his lap. "Oh, no!" If she could have self-destructed, she would have done so. Mortification and guilt, however, turned her to a pillar of salt. In response to conditioning programmed into her years earlier, she bowed her head, hiding her clenched fists under the table while she waited for the inevitable verbal lashing.

She deserved it. She was clumsy and cruel; she had no right to denigrate—

"Hey, Paige. Paige!"

A hand appeared in front of her face, fingers waggling back and forth. She focused on the strength of the fingers, visible through the chipped nails and reddened calluses. She couldn't lift her head.

"Paige, it was just a drink, and it was almost empty. It's okay, love. Look at me, please. It's okay."

Her head lifted with an effort, and she gazed blindly at the second button of his shirt.

"I know you didn't mean what you said. Neither did I. We're both exhausted and afraid, and probably punch-drunk." His finger slid under her chin and lifted it, and he sucked in his breath. "Don't look like that!" With his other hand he had been mopping up the drink with napkins, and tossed the sodden paper onto the table so abruptly Paige jerked as if he'd slapped her.

"He did this to you, didn't he?"

The low, rumbling tone brushed against her ears like the cold breath of an arctic wind. Startled out of her trance-like pose, Paige's eyes jerked up, widening at the threat emanating from the man sitting so still across from her. His shoulders were rigid, and a muscle in his jaw twitched as if he were grinding his teeth. His eyes. . . .

Paige's breath caught.

"You're sitting there like a little pup, waiting for the master's boot to kick it into submission. Just like this afternoon, in the woods, when you were convinced you were a worthless coward. Is that what your husband did to you? Did he twist the concept of wifely submission to an all time low, Paige?"

The paralysis of her vocal chords broke. "No! He wasn't like that. It wasn't—" she stopped, suddenly trembling. It had been exactly like that. "I should have handled it better than I did," she said painfully.

Jonah's hands reached back across to cover hers, stilling their betraying, restless movements. "A Christian man," he said softly, "is instructed to love his wife as Christ loved the church. If he didn't give you any of that, Paige, the fault was in your husband—not you."

He helped her to her feet, but stayed her with a hand on her arm when she would have started toward the door. "First thing in the morning, why don't we look up Justeen Gilroy's address, than pay her a visit?"

Paige looked blankly at him. "Who?"

One blunt finger tapped the end of her nose. "Your suggestion, remember? Justeen's the lady who donated Major Pettigrew's uniform. And yes, he was her father. I think she lives in North Carolina. A very pleasant lady, as I recall. Should make a nice change from our last few interviews."

He looked down, hands warm on her shoulders, and winked. Paige felt, at last, a little of her ice-encrusted heart beginning to melt.

CHAPTER 17

Justeen Gilroy lived in a sprawling frame house in a small town an hour west of Raleigh. She insisted on plying Jonah and Paige with cider, fresh-baked bread, and homemade preserves.

"I'm so glad you came, though goodness knows if I can be much help." She whipped off her apron, then sat down at the table with them. "That old trunk with Daddy's stuff gathered dust in the attic for thirty-odd years. I reckon Mama plumb forgot about it."

"Mm. We thought visiting in person might be worth a try." Jonah slowly retrieved the list of names from his shirt pocket and handed it to Justeen. "We found this behind the ribbons bar of your father's dress uniform."

The faded brown eyes sharpened. "Hmph. You don't say." She scanned the list, then gave it back. "I'm sorry—none of them ring any bells. Behind the ribbons, you say? I wonder what on earth they were doing there."

Just then a loud cheerful voice called through the back porch door, "Yoo-hoo! Justeen? You home?"

Justeen rolled her eyes. "That's my next door neighbor."

Nodding, Paige and Jonah rose. "We'll be going, then," Jonah said.

"I'm sorry I couldn't be more help. If I think of something, is there any way I can reach you? I plan to finish going through Mama's attic before winter. She was such a packrat. There's no telling what other goodies might surface." She gazed at Jonah with fascination. "It must be so exciting, being a writer and all."

Jonah hesitated. Paige glanced at him, then smiled at Justeen. "We're in and out so much that I think it would be better if I just gave you a call in a week or two. Would that be okay?"

"Sure. 'Bye now."

Neither spoke until they were back in their rental car.

"Well, that was a bust."

"I enjoyed meeting Justeen. She was so *normal* compared to all our other interviews."

"Normal. Such a nondescript word. . . ." Jonah sat loosely behind the steering wheel on their way back to the airport. "So far, everyone we've seen has a reason *not* to commit any nefarious crimes—and the same reason *to* commit a crime, if buying silence was the motive behind killing Professor K."

"Both Armand Gladstone and Patrick Minton are government reps. The way the media is nowadays, it seems pretty certain both of them would keep their noses as clean as possible."

"Covington's bucking for a judgeship."

"What about Brewster, then? Covington's father? He's already committed one crime."

"Over forty years ago. That doesn't make him a criminal now, but at this point I suppose he's also a viable choice."

Paige crumbled up a piece of paper. She was tired, edgy, and simmering with frustration. "Do you honestly think a man living in a dinky little house like that would have the money to hire a hit man?"

"Mm. . ." Jonah replied, his usual response when he was

thinking. "Were the funds he. . .um. . .'appropriated' ever recovered?"

"I don't know." She started ripping the crumpled paper into little pieces, until Jonah caught her wrist and tugged one hand into his.

"We'll work it out, Paige. Eventually, we'll work it out. Quit kicking against the pricks so, love." His hand toyed with her fingers. "Let's give it a rest and stop for a spot of supper, hmm? You've been playing Sherlock Holmes ever since the plane landed six hours ago."

"I'm not hungry."

He pressed down on her knee, stilling the jerking of her leg. "When you talk like that, your tummy's inches away from revolt. This place looks as good as any. Let's stop here. You'll feel better after."

Paige yanked her hand free. "Don't patronize me!" she snapped. Then, eyes stricken with horror and remorse, she retreated until the car door forced her to stop. "I'm sorry," she whispered.

Jonah ran his hand around the back of his neck, as he pulled the car into the restaurant parking lot and switched off the engine. Carefully removing his glasses, he stuffed them in his shirt pocket. "Are you expecting me to retaliate now? Have a slanging match? Is that how your husband would have responded?"

Paige's shoulders lifted in a tight little shrug.

"Tell me, when you were growing up, before you married, how did you handle displays of temper—whether your own or someone else's?" He took his glasses back out and started twirling them, head tilted to one side. He looked curious, genuinely interested, and disconcertingly non-threatening.

The corner of Paige's mouth twitched. "I usually laughed. Daddy used to say when I laughed I sounded like hens cackling, and how could anyone be angry listening to a bunch of chattering old biddies?"

Jonah's hand cupped her chin. "Then remember what your father used to say—not David." The fingers, warm and strong, stroked a light path down her throat, then dropped away. "I'd give anything to hear you laugh like that."

He turned then and opened the car door. "Let's go eat. We've a plane to catch in a couple of hours."

Paige spent the next few days with her nose buried in the galleys, trying to forget Jonah's words. Jonah, she knew, was either pursuing nebulous leads on his own—or working on a rough draft of his book. Under other circumstances, it would have been a peaceful, almost relaxing time. Seeing a book take shape, knowing she had contributed, normally filled her with deep satisfaction. Professor K had been so proud.

But the professor was dead, and Paige was hiding in a hotel room under lock and key, not knowing from minute to minute who might knock on the door.

Or worse, who might not bother to knock.

Guilt also struggled to swamp her at odd moments; she fought the familiar but unwanted emotion with the same gritty resolution as she did the fear and sadness.

It wasn't her fault Professor Kittridge had stumbled onto something that precipitated his murder.

It wasn't her fault, either, that the unknown murderer was now stalking her and Jonah.

It wasn't her fault that the professor's home had burned to the ground, destroying potential leads.

It wasn't her fault—but she still felt. . .responsible.

David would have gone to great lengths to make sure those feelings of guilt turned into a crushing millstone about her neck. He would have convinced her that *everything* was her fault, her responsibility.

Jonah had not.

Paige shoved aside a galley and rolled off the bed where she'd been working. She tugged on her hair with restless fingers that ended up tracing the contours of her ears—just like Jonah had that time. *What does he want from me? Everything's changed. I'm not comfortable with him anymore—and yet when I'm not with him, I feel so lost. So empty.*

With an irritated sigh she headed for the bathroom, hoping a long shower would relax her mind as well as her muscles.

When she finished, she moved from the bed to the round table by the window to resume working on the galleys.

Fifteen minutes later she let out a triumphant whoop, then clapped her hands over her mouth. Shoving back the chair, she headed for the phone, praying that Jonah was in his room by now.

"I think I've found them!" she all but screeched when, thankfully, he answered. "It was *Metter*, Georgia—not Medder. That's why we never found anything on that one name I remembered."

"Slow down, love," Jonah responded with such infuriating absentmindedness Paige snorted in exasperation.

"Jonah, remove yourself from the 1940s and *listen*. I'm trying to tell you I've found another clue, probably the most important one."

"Mm—sorry." He sighed heavily. "What did you find?"

"Never mind," Paige said sweetly. "I can tell you're involved in your book. I'll get hold of this address and fly down to Georgia, and you can—"

"I'll be there in a sec." There was a pause, then he added softly, "You little tease. You'll pay for that."

CHAPTER 18

Thirty seconds later he tapped on the door, and strolled into the room with the nonchalance of a tiger pretending to ignore a grazing gazelle. He was twirling his glasses, his coppery hair impossibly shaggy.

Paige grinned. "Sorry," she stated with cheerful unrepentance. "I know it's hard to surface now that you're finally writing."

"So you should be," Jonah growled. "It was finally starting to come together, and now my concentration is shot to Sussex and back."

The excitement and humor fizzled. "I didn't mean—I am sorry."

He studied her a minute in silence, then emitted an explosive sigh and flopped down into one of the chairs by the table where she'd been working, tossing his glasses on the pile of paper. "It's okay. What you're doing is just as important— probably more so."

"Only if you're interested in solving a real mystery."

"You don't have to clothe yourself in your chilly professional armor. Tell me what you've learned, Paige."

Paige bit her lip, then told him evenly, "I found the names of some of the P.O.W.s Professor K interviewed without me. One of them is James Denmark—from Georgia. I think that's the name I couldn't read in the professor's notes I found before they burned in the fire." She began tidying the galley pages. "I thought if we interviewed him, maybe we'd find out what was bothering the professor—and why he was murdered."

Jonah's hand reached over casually and covered hers. The clasp was gentle, but Paige couldn't move. She slanted him a sideways look, then dropped her gaze in confusion.

"I'm the one who should be sorry. What you're doing is infinitely more important." He squeezed her hand. "Forgive me, *min vacker radjur?*"

Paige swallowed hard, trying without success to free her hand. "Not if you don't stop calling me those names—or at least have the decency to start translating them."

She darted him another quick look and watched the irresistible grin inch across his face.

"You wouldn't like it."

"Probably not. Tell me anyway. I'd rather not like it in English."

"Mmph. I'll tell you if you'll tell me something in return."

"What?" Wary, immediately defensive again, Paige composed her features.

Jonah released her hand, sliding his fingers over hers so that the release was more of a caress. Leaning over, he whispered softly, "It's Swedish—and it means 'my pretty deer.' Now—tell me what your worm of a husband did to you that makes you wither in front of my eyes whenever you feel like you've done something wrong."

He deliberately tucked her hair behind her ear, his fingers brushing against the contours with delicate precision. Tiny flames leaped out of his eyes and snared her, surrounding her with heat and a relentless will as he wordlessly dared her to cover the ear.

His translation filled her with a strange warmth; his actions—and his demand—froze the blood in her veins. "It's reaction," she admitted jerkily. "I'm trying to outgrow it. . . ."

"You're doing fine. So talk to me—" His gaze flicked briefly to the galleys, "—then we'll discuss your discovery. But before we go on any more sleuthing trips, you're going to tell me about your marriage."

His voice was deceptively mild, and Paige's hands lifted automatically before their gazes met again. Slowly, her hands dropped back to the chair arms.

"I—all right." As she talked, her grip on the chair arms tightened. "I met David when I was twenty-one. We were members of the same church. He was considered quite a catch—successful lawyer, several years older than me, a church deacon, Sunday School teacher—the perfect Christian."

She was still looking across at Jonah, but she wasn't seeing him anymore.

"I'd been working at the Museum of American History for a year—loving it. But I loved David more. Or," she swallowed hard, "I thought I did. He wanted me to quit working because he said God had blessed him with enough wealth to support us both. And Christian wives are supposed to stay at home, be. . . submissive. I wanted to be a good Christian wife. . . ."

"Paige—"

Her eyes focused on him briefly. "You wanted to know. Let me finish while I can." She lifted her hands, flexing them as she stared at the bare ring finger of her left hand. "Within six months I learned that I could never be the perfect Christian wife David demanded. I can't sing—but I joined the choir because he said it set a good example. I joined every organization at church, volunteered for every project. If the church doors were open, I was there. I even taught a primary Sunday School class."

She was breathing faster, the words tumbling out in a chilling monotone. "It wasn't enough. I was supposed to be a perfect homemaker, too. Immaculate house—but no maid. I didn't have a job, after all. There was no reason why I couldn't keep the house straight. It was huge—four thousand square feet—his family home. We were going to have lots of children. But we didn't—David couldn't. He blamed me for that, too. . . ." Her voice cracked. "He said I couldn't do anything right. Eventually, I believed him."

"Why?"

Paige laughed, then ground her teeth together to stop the bitter sound. Jonah sounded almost angry. It was so unlike him. Or rather, it was so unlike the Jonah she thought she knew. Now if it had been David. . . .

She stood, pacing the room like a wild animal behind the bars of a zoo cage. "We were Christians. Our marriage was supposed to be Christ-centered. My husband was the head of the family. My parents have a wonderful marriage—I wanted mine to be the same. I thought if only I tried hard enough, I'd please him. He'd be proud of me."

"Did he beat you, Paige?"

She turned back to him, shocked. "No! He didn't. He wasn't abusive like that."

"There's all kinds of abuse," Jonah muttered.

"That's what Daddy tried to tell me after David died."

"How did he die?"

She collapsed back in the chair opposite Jonah. "I came home late from a church meeting one night. David was pacing the floor. He'd lost a case. . .had a fender-bender on the way home. . . and then I wasn't there." She lifted tortured eyes to Jonah. "I wasn't there. He was angry. So angry. Worse than usual. He yelled. It was all my fault. I tried to make up for coming home late. I promised to make his supper, take care of the car the next day. . . ."

Jonah leaned over, took her hands between his. "What happened then?"

"He. . .he just got angrier. He had a terrible temper. His face was all red, except the tips of his ears. . .and his nose—they always turned white." She closed her eyes, clinging to Jonah without even being aware of it. "He s-stopped so abruptly and looked at me. I'll never forget that look. Then he collapsed on the carpet. They told me later he died almost instantly. It was a stroke, caused by an aneurysm of the main vessel going to his brain—I forget the term. His father died the same way, I think."

"And you've been blaming yourself ever since." Jonah shook her hands. "Look at me, Paige."

"If I'd been a better Christian, I—mph—"

He kissed her, a hard, brief kiss that effectively stemmed the self-recriminating flow of words.

"If you'd been a 'better' Christian, you would have understood that God's concept of marriage does not mean that the wife is a doormat, an unpaid servant begging for the crumbs of her husband's approval."

"How would you know?" She lifted the back of her hand to her mouth, rubbing the still tingling lips. "How many times have *you* been married?"

"None." He tugged her fist away and dropped another kiss on the knuckles. "But I'm widely read—and widely traveled. And I have a very close Friend. I've read everything He ever said—including His words on the subject of marriage." He hesitated, then added with a roughness that prickled Paige's skin, "The woman I marry won't ever have to cower from me or wear herself to the bone trying to live up to some set of rules I demand."

He looked at Paige. "The woman I marry will know she is loved—every day, every way."

Paige suddenly felt overwhelmingly bereft, empty. "I—see. Have you—do you plan to get married soon, then?" He hadn't mentioned anything about a woman. Pain, rapier sharp and white hot, suddenly ripped through her heart.

112

Jonah's face went blank. "I doubt it. There's too much going on in my life right now to pursue the matter." He reached over and scooped up the notes Paige had made. "Especially when some idiots out there want to speed our entrance through the pearly gates. Tell me what you've found, but Paige—" He waited until Paige lifted her gaze back to his, "—don't confuse me with David again. I don't like it."

Paige lifted her chin. "Then don't confuse me with your dream woman and kiss me again. I don't like *it*."

Up went a corner of his moustache. "Don't worry, little *chate*, when we kiss, I know who you are."

Fiery color burned her cheeks, and she snatched the papers from his grasp. "The man's name is James Denmark, and he lives in Metter, Georgia. It shouldn't be too difficult to find his address. I plan to fly down as soon as possible. You can come if you want to."

"Wouldn't miss it."

"The matter of your former employee has been seen to."

"Excellent. How soon can I expect to hear of similar success with the woman and her writer friend?"

"These matters must be planned with meticulous care. Your former employee was a bungler, very clumsy. He made them wary, suspicious, so I will have to be extra careful."

"I told you they're at the Castille. The information—"

"I am aware of your requirements and your timetable. You are aware that your demands introduce a higher level of risk than a simple matter of elimination."

"I cannot risk any loose ends. Not now."

"The matter will be seen to—but patience is a much desired virtue."

CHAPTER 19

James Denmark—or Jimmy, as he requested—lived with his wife and three children in a neat brick ranch house with four columns supporting the front porch. It was a sullen November day, with a washed-out gray sky and barren trees rattling in the wet, chilly breeze.

Paige and Jonah talked to Jimmy in a cluttered family room, for which his sweet-voiced wife apologized effusively as she raced around picking up toys and unfolded laundry. She finally scuttled out the door to return to work, and Jimmy watched her through the window, his long bony face both affectionate and bitter.

"She wears herself down somethin' fierce, 'cuz I can't work much." He shook his head, then maneuvered his wheelchair back to Paige and Jonah. "Not too many jobs 'round here for a man with only one leg."

"Mr. Denmark—Jimmy," Paige sat down across from him and smiled. "Like I explained to you last night, I've been helping compile character profiles of Vietnam P.O.W.s for a book being written by various individuals for the American History Association. You, apparently, were one of the ones Professor Kittridge—that's who I worked with—interviewed."

"Yeah. . .I remember. Professor Kittridge, huh? Don't re-collect the name, but I remember him. Nice old geezer, but pretty strange. He mumbled most of the time I was telling him 'bout my wartime experiences." Watery blue eyes shifted from Paige to Jonah, then back to Paige. "He asked me about some guy—can't place my tongue around his name right off either—I'd never heard of him. I told him to try Slicks—that's my buddy. He lives in Eastman now. Don't know whether he ever did or not, but I can give Slicks a call if you like."

"If we showed you a list of names, do you think you'd recognize the one the professor asked about?" Jonah asked casually.

"Nah—the docs told me it's probably from my war injuries—but I don't remember names and stuff too well anymore, even some of my favorite ballplayers."

"Perhaps seeing them. . . ." Paige handed him a list of typed names. "Do any of those look at all familiar?"

They held their breath while Jimmy scanned the list, but in the end he shook his head. "Nope. Nothin' rings a bell." He handed the list back to Paige. "That old professor, now, he said he'd go on over to Slicks'. I reckon you'll have to do the same. You say my name's gonna be in that book? What a hoot!"

With commendable restraint, Jonah persuaded Jimmy to call Slicks to make sure he was going to be home. Eastman, he found from studying the map with Paige while Jimmy was on the phone, was about a two hour drive southwest of Metter. He groaned, and Paige lifted her head, smiling ruefully.

"Another goose chase. . ."

"Maybe not," Paige offered with the quirky little half smile that made Jonah want to kiss the uplifted corner. "At least we know this was one of the places Professor K visited. We have to be getting close. Remember how almost fearful he was that last day? How withdrawn and secretive?"

"I remember," Jonah folded the map up and laid it back on the table. Every instinct honed over the years was screaming at him. "On to Eastman, then."

115

"Slicks can't wait to talk to you." Jimmy wheeled back into the room, face alight with excitement. "He wants to know if ya'll have enough evidence this time to convict the scum bag who set him and the boys in Company C up. Now I remember. Slicks said the name."

"That's it. The Vietnam connection." Paige murmured half to herself an hour later. "He might have behaved like a politician, but he was so *nice*."

Jonah grinned in the gathering darkness of the car. "People say Hitler loved little children." He pretended to cower when Paige swatted his arm. "Let's not condemn the man without hearing what this Slicks fellow has to say."

"The professor was convinced. I bet that's why he was so subdued on the flight back to D.C. He knew he would be opening a can of worms."

"Let's hope we have better luck than the professor did," Jonah observed with terse finality. He glanced across. "Are you sure you won't consider flying home to Kansas?"

"I'm have too much fun in the land of Oz," Paige retorted with enough flippancy to tell Jonah that she was petrified. He caught a corner of his moustache between his teeth and chewed.

"If we get any kind of evidence, I'm going back to the police."

"The man's apparently got enough contacts in the right places to hire goons to do his dirty work. I don't think he's going to let us just waltz into the police station. I'm still amazed that we made it down here without being followed."

"Mm. Do you trust me?"

He waited for almost a mile before she replied and the choking band of tension tightening his chest could relax. "Yes, I trust you." Spoken in a soft voice, with her face carefully averted—but at least she was willing to admit it. They weren't

116

back yet to their old relationship of easy professional camaraderie, and Paige's gaze still tended to skitter from his chin to his brow and points beyond, but slowly, surely, she was relaxing in his presence again.

Jonah reached out his arm, momentarily resting his hand on one fragile shoulder, and counted himself blessed. "We're on the side of the angels, love," he promised. "God willing, we'll find enough muck to stick to the blighter, and maybe Professor K can rest in peace. Then, you and I can return to the—ah—humdrum world of fiction!"

Slicks met them at the door of the filthiest American apartment Jonah had ever had the misfortune to visit. Tall, skinny to the point of emaciation, Slicks acted oblivious to the mess, waving them eagerly toward a sagging card table laden with yellowing newspapers.

They had barely crossed the threshold when Slicks started filling their ears with his opinion of a certain politician; every other word was an unprintable obscenity. Jonah gave Paige what he hoped was an encouraging smile, then turned to Slicks. "Can I have a word with you in private?" he requested, interrupting the other man's rank opinion of the man's ancestors.

"Uh—sure."

He led Jonah down a narrow hall and into a bedroom littered with clothes. Jonah lifted a brow, reached past the puzzled Slicks, and shut the door.

They returned to Paige a few moments later "Now," Jonah divided his attention between Slicks and the table covered with newspapers, "why don't you tell us what you told Professor Kittridge."

Slicks began to talk, expletives deleted. Jonah caught Paige's astonished, hastily concealed amusement, and winked at her.

"I was a grunt in the First Cavalry—we were s'posed to clean out a nest of Viet Cong." He spat. "Humph! Some C.O. The lieutenant gave us the coordinates, then sent us ahead." Slicks fumbled in the papers, tugged one out and handed it to Jonah. "That's *his* story there."

Jonah scanned the twenty-odd year old article, which praised one Lieutenant Armand Gladstone for his fearless courage in trying to recover his men from an ambush. He was tragically unable to succeed, and over half his unit was killed or captured. Gladstone himself was wounded and received a Purple Heart. Details were on page sixteen. Jonah looked back at Slicks. "What's your version, since I gather it isn't the one here in the paper?"

Slicks opened his mouth, glanced across at Paige, and hastily closed it on a gulp. "The one in the paper's a crock—the whole thing's a crock. He didn't rescue us, man—he sold us down the river."

"What?" Paige gasped.

Jonah carefully lifted a wrinkled shirt and a pile of magazines from a straightback chair and gestured for Paige to sit down. "Why," he asked Slicks, "didn't you bring the matter to the authorities when you finally made it home?"

Slicks shot him a look full of bitterness, disillusionment, and decades of pain. "It was '73 by the time I finally made it home, and ol' Gladstone was sittin' purty. The whole state bragged on the war hero. Made me puke." He looked for a moment at the pile of papers, his eyes burning. "He'd been home close to three years by then—honorably discharged, of course. Probably bribed who knows all to git that Bronze Medal. And already elected to the state legislature. You think some dumb old private who looked like a dead man and didn't have two dirty kleenex of his own's going to influence public opinion?"

"Why didn't you try?" Paige burst out passionately.

Jonah eyed her out of the corner of his eyes. She was wringing her hands, practically ready to fly out of the chair. The gray eyes shot sparks. Jonah sighed. She was ready to skewer Armand Gladstone and hang him out to dry; he hoped he could calm her down before they returned to Washington. "Why didn't you?" he repeated mildly to Slicks. "A lot of villainy occurred during that war. I'm sure someone would have listened to you."

"I ain't no fool. People like Gladstone don't turn the other cheek. It was still my word agin' his—and you can figure how *that* would have turned out."

"So why did you bring it up when Professor Kittridge came to talk to you?" Paige asked.

Slicks hunched his shoulders, eyeing her suspiciously. Jonah cleared his throat. When Paige glanced across, he shook his head slightly, smiling a little. She grimaced and relaxed back in her chair. "I'm sorry, Mr. Slicks. I didn't mean to browbeat. It's just that the professor was. . .the professor died this past August."

Slicks shrugged. "Sorry to hear it. As I recall, he didn't look so hot the day he came here. Main reason I talked to the old man was he promised he'd found another ex-P.O.W. whose story more or less matched mine. Said he was writing a book and that he wanted to tell the truth. I guess he ain't writin' no more, huh?" He wiped a trembling hand across his mouth and eyes. "I gotta have a drink. Ya'll want a drink?"

"I think," Jonah spoke carefully into the silence before Paige had a chance to, "that if you could perhaps remember the name of that other P.O.W., we'll just be on our way. . . ."

CHAPTER 20

"What do *you* suggest we do?" Paige gathered up all their notes and stuffed them back in her portfolio, the motions short, jerky. She stifled the urge to grind her teeth at Jonah, who sprawled beside her at a still damp picnic table, legs stretched lazily in front of him. He was chewing on the stem of a weed and dreamily contemplating the clear deep blue of the November sky after a drenching rain.

They had spent a restless night at a seedy roadside motel to avoid driving after dark in a pounding rainstorm. They were now on their way to catch a late afternoon flight out of Atlanta. Paige had been up since dawn, poring over her notes and pacing the floor, urgency tugging at her with clawing fingers.

And Jonah, who had knocked on her door around eight looking rested, relaxed and fit, refused to drive any faster than a sedate fifty-five. When he pulled into a scenic rest stop on a deserted stretch of I-16, announcing that they had plenty of time before their flight, Paige wanted to scream.

"I still say that after we visit Andrew McPhearson, we'll have something to show the police."

With a suspiciously long-suffering sigh, Jonah sat up. "Paige," he tossed the weed away and studied her with gentle, but frighteningly implacable eyes, "I think I better make something a little clearer to you than I'd prefer."

Paige shifted uneasily. "What do you mean?"

He seemed to hesitate, and she knew she wasn't going to like what she heard.

"We weren't followed down here because we managed to give our watchdog the slip—remember razzing me for sneaking out the service entrance, just in case? But if Armand Gladstone *is* behind the professor's murder—and it looks likely—then he knows where we've been hiding—and where we're likely to be visiting." His fist pounded softly on the table. "We've offered ourselves on a silver platter."

"We knew all along there was a chance we'd happen onto a murderer." *But you didn't really believe it, did you? You thought of it as just more research. . .an extension to Jonah's book. Paige, how could you be such a dummy?*

"We'll never make it to the police station, will we?" She sat woodenly on the damp bench, worrying over possibilities until Jonah startled her out of her preoccupation by placing his hand on hers.

"Don't pack it up. That's why we're stopped here."

He moved his hand, pretending not to notice her heightened color.

"Plotting strategy?" Paige quipped. Drat it all. Why did her leg have to jig about like that, anyway? She'd always hated the betraying signal. Crossing her legs, she propped her elbows on her knees. "Why can't we go straight to the police from the airport?"

"I'd considered that. The trouble is, I understand how Professor K felt—I have a distinct reluctance to start smearing the name of an eminently respected Congressman without some pretty substantial evidence."

"What do you call Slicks and, hopefully, Andrew Mc-Phearson?"

"Two unknown men who've kept silent about the matter twenty years. And in an election year, their motives for suddenly spilling the beans would automatically be suspect." He stood abruptly. "We need something more." He looked down at Paige. "We need to be able to prove that the man or men who are trying to kill us, who torched the professor's house, and who searched our apartments, are doing so under Armand Gladstone's orders."

Paige made an elaborate play of examining her fingernails. "I don't see how we can," she eventually observed without looking at Jonah, "unless we can trap them into compromising themselves. . .before they can kill us off."

"I'm aware of that," Jonah shot back with biting British sarcasm. Suddenly his arms shot out and hauled Paige to her feet and into his embrace. He spoke hoarsely, burying his face in her hair. "I'm all *too* aware of that."

Paige trembled, wanting to pull back, yet wanting to surrender and cling. Her heart hammered a frantic tattoo against her ribs when Jonah's hands slid beneath her hair. The long fingers cupped her head, holding it so that she had no choice but to meet the stormy blue depths of his gaze. Her hands slowly found their way around his waist. With a broken sigh, she closed her eyes.

"Paige," he whispered in a husky voice. His mouth nuzzled behind her ear, her temple, down her jaw as he murmured incoherent words and phrases in a mixture of languages. "Paige. . ."

She had never felt like this before, even in the first euphoric weeks of her courtship with David. She wanted to submerse herself in Jonah's warmth, in the shelter of his arms—yet she didn't feel swamped. . .overwhelmed. She didn't feel swept away in a man's towering passion she was helpless to control.

She was in the middle of a fire—but the fire itself protected her, cherished her.

All the brittleness, all the lacquer of a facade carefully built and buttressed over the past years began to crumble, falling away in the sweeping tide of pulsing warmth flooding through her. When Jonah's mouth finally covered hers, Paige melted against him, her arms holding him every bit as fiercely as he held her.

Eventually Jonah lifted his head, resting his forehead against hers. "This isn't exactly the strategy I had in mind," he murmured, laughter running through the words.

Paige hugged him, basking in the warmth, the strength emanating from him. How could she ever have been afraid of Jonah? "Well, we still face a life-threatening situation," she teased. "That *is* the only condition under which you can kiss me, isn't it?"

"What would happen if I admitted I don't mind kissing you under any conditions?"

For some reason, his just-as-teasing rejoinder triggered an uncomfortable memory of the other day, when she had shared the story of her marriage.

And Jonah had talked of the woman he would someday marry.

Paige stiffened and removed her arms, stepping away. When Jonah would have pulled her back, she eluded him with the grace of a will-o-the-wisp.

"Paige?"

"I forgot," Paige spoke in carefully unaccented tones, "that somewhere in the wings, there's a woman waiting. The one you promised would feel loved. . .every day."

Jonah inhaled, the heavy brows drawing together above the suddenly piercing eyes of a raptor. "There's no woman waiting in the wings," he promised softly, with utter sincerity, belying the fierce expression on his face. "I was merely sharing my own feelings. You had just finished baring your soul to me, Paige. I wanted you to know—on a deep subconscious level you never have to question—that I could never treat a woman the way your husband did you."

Paige opened her mouth, then closed it. He was looking at her so intently she felt a fine trembling shiver through her limbs all over again.

"You still don't understand, do you?" Jonah said after a minute. He raised his eyes heavenward, reached out, then abruptly stuffed his hands in the pockets of his cords. "Paige... there's more at stake than our relationship here. It's important—vitally important—that you trust me. Trust me so implicitly that, like Isaac and Abraham, if I held a knife ready to plunge into your heart, you'd still look up at me with trust."

"I trust Jesus Christ like that," Paige replied slowly. "And my parents. But I don't know if I can ever again trust a man that blindly."

"If you can't trust me like that, you may get us both killed." The blunt word fell between them like stones. "I didn't urge you to tell me about your marriage just to exorcise David and free you from your past, although I hope it did that." The flickering smile was more a movement beneath the moustache, over so quick Paige wasn't sure she'd seen it. "Like I told you before—I have to know you. I have to know how you react under life-threatening circumstances." He sighed heavily. "I have to know, if I tell you to jump, and it's pitch black so you have no idea where you're jumping, whether or not you'll jump anyway—because you trust me—or whether you'll freeze. And end up with a bullet in your back."

Paige gazed at him with tortured eyes. Vignettes flashed through her brain like snapshots in a child's viewfinder: Jonah, the day she met him, looking diffident and very British in his heather-green sweater, glasses slipping off his nose while he petitioned for her help; Jonah, gently shutting a book she'd been scouring for research and hauling her off to dinner in the manner of a small boy sheepishly requesting a treat; Jonah, smiling that slow smile, eyes twinkling as he called her one of

124

those ridiculous foreign endearments, just to rattle her; Jonah roaring up to Professor K's office on his Harley-Davidson motorcycle, looking incongruously like an absentminded professor while he explained to Paige that he loved the bike but hated the noise so he had had the engine modified.

Jonah dispatching a criminal twice his size with the ease of a trained professional.

Jonah.

"I'm trying," she promised, her voice cracking. "I'm trying, Jonah."

A bleak look entered his eyes. "It's not enough," he stated flatly. "It's not enough."

Tears welled up, and Paige blinked furiously to keep them from spilling. Ducking her head, she grabbed the portfolio.

"Paige?"

She stopped, keeping her back to him. "Yes?" The tears crowded her throat, strangling the word. She gripped the portfolio tighter.

"I plan to win that trust." She felt something stir her hair, like the merest breath of a breeze. "Just like I plan to keep you safe."

Paige tried to take a breath. "I know you will."

She started back to the car, and Jonah fell in beside her. He held the door open, and Paige started to climb in, still with averted face. His next words froze her, for they were—unbelievably—laced with that unmistakable thread of dry humor.

"I plan to pray a lot, too, of course. I'd hate for you to labor under the misapprehension that I have too high an opinion of my abilities." He paused, then added even more dryly, "And I'd hate for the Lord to teach me a lesson in humility on the matter, which as I'm sure you know, He does very well."

CHAPTER 21

After landing in D.C., they took a taxi to yet another hotel, this time one of the chains off I-95 on the Virginia side. Jonah phoned the Castille and arranged for their belongings to be packed and sent over. Then he called the detective with whom he'd maintained contact.

Paige, exhausted from travel, tension, and the tenuous relationship with Jonah, slipped next door to her room, flopped down across the bed, and fell asleep.

Hours later the phone woke her. "Yes?" she answered sleepily, yawning as she sat up.

"Paige? Our luggage is here. I'll trot down and pick it up to avoid letting anyone know what rooms we're in."

"Mmm. . ."

"I woke you, didn't I? I'm sorry, love." His voice was contrite, and around another jaw-popping yawn, Paige hurried to reassure him.

"I shouldn't have fallen asleep like that anyway. I'll come down to the lobby with you so you don't have to carry everything by yourself."

"I'd rather you didn't. I can manage fine. The only reason I rang you was so you wouldn't be frightened when I knocked on your door."

"I think I'd like to stretch my legs anyway. I appreciate the gesture, but I'll meet you in the lobby." She hung the phone up, rose, and rummaged under the bed for her shoes. That was the only reason, she told her reflection in the mirror, for the

126

abrupt wash of color in her cheeks.

When she opened the door, Jonah stood in front of her, waiting with folded arms. "You're being difficult," he pronounced with lazy humor.

Paige moved into the hallway, checked the door to be sure it was locked, and shoved the key into the pocket of her slacks. "I won't be coddled."

"Mmph."

The young man who had brought their luggage from the Castille was waiting impatiently in the lobby, shifting from one foot to the other. "Thanks, man," he muttered when Jonah passed him a generous tip. He nodded to Paige, then headed out the door.

Paige idly wondered how fast he'd spend the twenty dollar bill, then turned to help Jonah. "Does it look like everything's there?"

"Two suitcases, two hang-up bags, my shaving kit, and your cosmetic case."

"Where's my briefcase? The galleys were in there."

They searched frantically, but the burgundy leather briefcase was nowhere to be found. Paige and Jonah regarded each other grimly. "I *knew* I should have taken it with me," Paige groaned. "But we were just going to be gone that one night. . . ." She shook her head. "What do you think: Oversight—or planned?"

"I'll find out," Jonah promised. "Let's get this stuff to our rooms, and I'll get over to the Castille. If I use the service entrance, maybe I won't be spotted."

"*We'll* go."

"I was going to take the Harley. I retrieved it earlier from the garage, while you were sleeping."

Paige stood her ground. "I'm responsible for those galleys. I'm coming."

"Fine," Jonah growled, "but you'd be safer here."

127

"I'll be taking a taxi—not your Harley," Paige shot back tartly. "I'll meet you there." She grabbed her suitcase and the cosmetic case and headed for the elevator.

Jonah argued with her up the elevator and down the corridor. Paige listened politely, not commenting, her face a bland mask. Ten minutes later she was back downstairs in the lobby, waiting for the taxi.

Jonah followed her to the Castille, or at least he would have if the cabbie hadn't run a yellow light a few blocks after they exited the beltway. Paige stifled her nagging conscience, and the twinge of uneasiness at being totally on her own for the first time in weeks. *You'd think I was a schoolgirl off to her first trip in the big city.* She felt silly sneaking in a side door, eyes shifting from side to side like a caricature in a spy-spoof.

The desk clerk at the Castille remembered her, and immediately called a bellboy to escort her to her old room. Paige hesitated, wondering if she should wait for Jonah. She opened her mouth to tell the bellboy, then stopped. She was being paranoid. Living on the edge these past few weeks had her seeing assassins behind every tree, suspicious intent in every eye. *This is not a good way to live, Lord. Forgive me.*

She would be careful, but she was through being afraid. She smiled at the bellboy, and followed him up the staircase to her old room. She wondered how long it would take Jonah to catch up and smiled to herself. Words between them were very likely going to fly thick and fast. How she ever could have considered him mild and easygoing was yet another mystery.

The prospect of confrontation brought anticipation instead of her knee-jerk shivering dread, and Paige almost froze in the middle of the staircase at the realization: She didn't feel cowed by the thought of Jonah disagreeing with her. In fact, not thirty minutes earlier, she had actually done what *she* wanted to do instead of what Jonah wanted her to do.

Heady stuff, that. By the time this whole mess was resolved, she might actually be a functioning human being again. She might even be able to go back to her old job at the Smithsonian. *Thank you, Lord, for Jonah, even if he can be the most understated bully I've ever known. . . .*

"Here we are, miss."

The bellboy unlocked the door and opened it, standing back so Paige could enter. "Thanks. I'll only be a minute."

"Take your time. No one's scheduled for this room tonight. Have a nice evening, miss." He headed back down the hall, whistling.

Paige started to call after him to wait, then caught herself. She'd only be here a couple of minutes. Hurrying in spite of the silent lecture, she began searching the room. Relief almost made her laugh aloud when she found the briefcase right where she'd left it, on the shelf above the clothes hangers. Whoever had packed her clothes had obviously—

"I knew that briefcase would bring one of you scurrying back. How fortunate for me it turned out to be you."

Paige cried out and jerked around, an icy avalanche of terror engulfing her. Her eyes fastened with paralyzed incredulity on the lithe sinuous form of an Oriental man dressed all in black. He stepped out of the bathroom and moved toward her, a knife in his hand. The point danced in front of Paige's face like a cobra poised to strike.

She lunged instinctively, trying to dodge past him so she could make it to the door. The man's foot shot out and sent her crashing to the floor, knocking the breath from her lungs. Then he was on her. Some sort of cloth sack was yanked completely over her head, then his hand gathered the edges and twisted. His other hand pressed the knife in her back.

"Do not be foolish," he hissed softly.

He dragged her to her feet and hauled her backward. Paige writhed, choking, her hands lifting to claw at the brutal hold on her neck. She was blind, unable to breathe, unable to hear

129

beyond the growing buzz that rang in her ears.

Pain suddenly slashed across the back of her hand.

"Do not move—or the next time it will be your throat." She was slammed down onto a chair. Her head was yanked back, the fist at her throat loosening a fraction—while the knife pressed a fraction harder on the other side. "Where's your friend?"

"He'll be here any minute." Paige felt disembodied, and heard her hoarse, barely audible voice as if it belonged to somebody else. She shifted, trying to escape the stranglehold and the shiny silver knife she knew would haunt her in nightmares. "You won't trap him as easily. . . ."

Paige gasped when the knife pressed harder. "Do not move or speak unless I tell you to," he warned.

Paige felt something warm trickle down the side of her neck, and a wave of blackness and nausea roiled through her.

"I think," the cold, emotionless voice continued from somewhere above and behind, "that I'll be able to persuade him to cooperate."

"What is it you want to know?"

Jonah's voice echoed in the suddenly quiet room. Paige heard a sudden hiss of surprise from the man behind her, and the knife jerked against her skin. She cringed away.

"Let her go, and I'll tell you what you want to know."

"I think you'll tell me what I want to know regardless, Mr. Sterling."

If he had sounded panicked, Paige would not have been as terrified as she was at hearing his precisely modulated voice calmly warn Jonah back. Fighting for breath, she tried to keep the buzzing blackness at bay so she could somehow help Jonah.

"Maybe so," Jonah responded with the same lack of emotion. "But if you hurt her more, I might forget that vengeance belongs to the Lord."

The man emitted a dry chuckle, like the sound of rattling skeletal bones. "I'm going to enjoy this more than I thought." His voice changed abruptly. "Now—the woman and I are going to walk out of here, nice and quiet, when it's just a little darker. It does not suit my purposes to kill you both here."

"Since you've already told us you plan to kill us, why should I let you do that without putting up some sort of fight? What have I got to lose?"

Into the scarlet and black swirling silence, Paige's heightened senses—raw with terror—could detect a subtle shift in the assailant's attitude. It wasn't uneasiness, but rather a thoughtfulness, a calculated weighing of options.

Beneath the suffocating folds of the sack, Paige closed her eyes, but it didn't help. She could still see the empty, dead pits of his almond eyes, the utterly expressionless face. Even more frightening than that was the chilling knowledge that this was most definitely *not* the man who had been stalking them earlier. Where was he?

The flat side of the knife caressed her throat, and her stomach clenched as she fought the gagging reflex.

"It will almost be a shame to kill you." Her assailant mused slowly to Jonah. "You display admirable courage, even though you have no choice."

"I'm sure you think so," Jonah murmured.

The fist at Paige's throat twisted viciously. "You are a dead man, Mr. Sterling. As is the woman. I would prefer to kill both of you now, but my employer unfortunately insists on securing information he is convinced you both have. It's a shame you didn't leave it in the briefcase. Then you'd already be dead— and I'd be gone. A pity."

"You won't get away."

Paige could detect nothing in Jonah's voice—no fear, no hopelessness. She needed to see. She needed to breathe without fighting for every strangulated breath. She needed to prove, just once, that *she* could be brave.

The cold handle of the knife touched her throat again. Paige closed her eyes.

"I am not the clumsy, stupid predecessor of my employer. The woman and I will walk out of here." The voice was tinged with impatience, the first sign of emotion Paige had heard. "You will check the corridor and make sure it is empty. And before you get any ideas, Mr. Sterling, your research assistant will die now—very painfully—if you're gone longer than five seconds."

Paige's eyes opened wide now, but the rough cloth over her head was too opaque, the blackness total. She was as trapped and helpless as a bird in a snare. She heard the sound of footsteps, then an opening door. She could hear the quiet breathing of the man behind her, as well as her own rasping, labored breaths. Her heartbeat counted each second, throbbing a relentless rhythm in her eardrums.

"The corridor's free."

The hand at her neck tugged upward. Paige rose, stumbling and awkward. The hand tightened.

"Just stand over there. . .that's far enough."

Paige was jerked backward, against the man's chest. The fist loosened its hold at last—but the arm holding the knife wrapped around her throat. She still couldn't breathe, couldn't move—couldn't see. She felt movement at her elbow and heard a slither of sound.

"A knife for Mrs. Hawthorne—and a bullet for you." His voice sharpened. "Stay back!"

"The sound of that gun will bring a lot of people," Jonah stated calmly.

A gun! No wonder Jonah hadn't tried anything. With just the knife, there might have been a chance. But a gun!

The man forced Paige forward. She dragged her steps as much as she dared, fighting panic at not being able to see

Jonah's eyes so she would know what he wanted her to do.

"Where are you taking me?" The words were garbled, strained. She wet her lips, tried again. "Where are you taking me?"

"Be quiet."

"Why don't you ask what you want to know and leave her here? I'll come with you as a hostage."

"No thank you, Mr. Sterling. My employer may be unaware of your many and varied. . .talents, but I am not."

"I hope Gladstone paid you up front."

"I don't know who you are talking about."

"Hey, lighten up—she's going to faint on you."

Part of Paige wished she *could* faint, but having the possibility pointed out redoubled her effort to avoid doing so. Maybe if she started talking, it would give Jonah more time to think. "We found witnesses," she breathed, forcing her limbs to relax. The blurring vortex of stars and blackness receded.

"No, Paige!" Jonah interjected. For the first time emotion colored his voice.

"Tell him. . .he's been exposed," Paige continued desperately. She had the man's attention—she could feel it. The arm around her throat slackened marginally. "I—I can write down their names. . ."

"You would just make up names. Do not waste my time." He moved forward, forcing Paige ahead. "Later, when we are alone—then you will tell me everything I want to know. I said don't move!"

The man holding her jerked and fired the gun. The terrifying explosion seared Paige's ears, deafening and deadly.

"Jonah!" she screamed. "Jonah, no! No!" Beyond fear, beyond hysteria, she threw herself backward, arms flailing, fingers arched like talons. Something hard slammed into the side of her head, and she hurtled into oblivion.

CHAPTER 22

The sound of the hotel door closing brought Jonah back to full awareness. He didn't move, didn't wince or try to take a much needed breath to signal that he was, in fact, alive.

His right temple burned and throbbed where the bullet had grazed him, but he ignored the pain. Slitting his eyes open just enough to see, he searched as much of the dark hotel room as he could without moving his head. There was nothing. No sense of anyone else present. Would someone investigate—or would they shrug the gunshot aside as a television on too loud or a car backfiring? The only sound he heard was the subdued roar of traffic in the street below.

The echo of Paige's anguished cry still ringing in his ears, Jonah surged to his feet. Swaying, he almost fell before he caught himself on the back of a chair. He had to follow them—now. Pain reverberated through his head in an anvil chorus, but he ignored it, terror for Paige goading him like a cat-o-nine-tail whip. Moving slowly, he opened the door, then ran lightly down the hall to the back stairs.

One flight below he heard the echoing slam of the door that exited into a narrow alley between the hotel and a cluster of brownstones. *Please, Lord. Don't let him kill her. . .please.*

He ran down the stairs, almost losing his balance again from the stabbing pain that lashed his forehead with each leaping step. He opened the door at the bottom slowly, carefully, wiping sweat and blood away with a shaking hand. From the front of the alley, he heard an engine roar to life.

Jonah sprinted toward the sound, staying hunched and in the shadows. Right now, the only thing that might be keeping Paige alive was the fact that her abductor had been just arrogant enough not to make sure Jonah was dead.

The man with whom Jonah had tangled on two other occasions had been hasty, even clumsy—like the Oriental assassin obviously hired as a replacement had observed. *But pride, you sorry piece of snake's belly, goes before destruction. And I plan to do everything I can to insure your destruction.*

As he reached the street, a van with an electrician's logo on the side was just pulling away. Jonah couldn't make out the license plate, but in the glare of a streetlight caught just enough of a glimpse of the driver to confirm his suspicions. He ran into the driveway in front of the hotel, straining his eyes to follow the taillights of the van.

The Harley was parked at the curb. Without hesitation, Jonah swung onto its back, crammed on his helmet—wincing at the fresh pain—and gunned the engine.

He followed the van carefully, petrified that its cold-blooded driver would catch sight of the Harley in the rearview mirror. He would know, of course, that Jonah rode one.

Twice he almost lost them in the welter of blinding lights, the confusion of the endless Washington traffic. The metallic taste of fear swelled up in his throat, choking him, receding only marginally when, both times, he was able to spot the van again.

The image of a terrified Paige filled his mind. She had been so calm, so brave in the hotel room, even though Jonah had almost been able to feel her panic. He wanted to tell her that, praise her for the strength he knew she had—that Paige herself couldn't see. . .now he might never get the chance.

Not even in the most reckless of his non-Christian years had Jonah known this level of terror. Paige—helplessly blind-folded, a knife to her throat, bleeding. . . .

I can't think about that now, Lord. Help me. Protect her. Please, Lord. Please. I know I was arrogant to think I could protect her. I knew all along that her protection—ours—came only from you. Forgive me, Lord, but let me be in time to help her. Please.

The van headed south on I-95, and Jonah followed, concealed behind a semi traveling about the same speed as the van. Twenty minutes later the van exited. Jonah pulled off at the top of the exit ramp and watched them turn right. Gunning the engine quickly, he followed them, maintaining a two block buffer, down a section of road flanked with fast-food restaurants, truck stops, filling stations, and a couple of motels.

The road narrowed to two lanes, winding out of sight into the darkness beyond the streetlights, neon signs, and businesses. Jonah turned off the headbeam on the modified Harley. . .and prayed.

About ten miles later the van turned again. Several hundred yards down a rough, county road, he pulled into the parking lot of an abandoned gas station. Jonah killed the engine of the Harley and coasted until he could pull the big machine over behind some trees. After dismounting, he turned the bike around, making sure it was well off the road but easily accessible. Then he made his way stealthily toward the van. Crouched low, he stayed in the shadows, slipping from cover to deeper cover.

A cold, white, three-quarter moon shed streamers of chilly light on the earth below. Walking on the balls of his feet to avoid any sound, he melted behind a convenient tree trunk when his ear caught the sound of a door opening. He shivered, abruptly feeling the stinging bite of a late autumn evening as a breeze ruffled his hair and rippled through the leafless branches of the trees.

Watching from ten yards away, his hands curled into fists at his sides as the man who had kidnapped Paige slid down, then opened the sliding panel doors. Reaching in, he hefted out her limp body, and for one shattered second Jonah froze, pain welling up with such agony that he had to balance himself against the rough bark of the tree trunk.

Then she moaned.

The faint trickle of sound riveted Jonah. His eyes followed the movements of the dark, amorphous shapes as they blended into one. Carrying her, the man disappeared around the side of the building.

Rage consumed Jonah. Rage, and the atavistic urge to destroy that which threatened someone he loved. He ran, his blood surging through his body in the same pounding rhythm as his soundless steps.

Two minutes later he was crouched beneath a window. The man had taken Paige inside the store and dumped her on the concrete floor. A kerosene lantern had been lit and placed on a dusty countertop. In the flickering light, the impassive Oriental stared at Paige, and even from the window Jonah could see the evil in his face.

Paige gained consciousness slowly, almost reluctantly. Her head felt as if someone had dropped a load of sandbags on it. An annoying stinging sensation in her neck, coupled with a sticky wetness, made her turn her head. The movement, though slight, was a mistake. She moaned in pain.

"Ah. You are awake."

The voice ripped through her muddled senses like a drop of acid on a hundred-year old piece of cloth. The hotel room. A killer with a knife. A gun. *Jonah.* Tears flooded her eyes and soaked her face. "You killed him," she choked out hoarsely, so crushed with the weight of her agony it barely registered that the sack had been removed from her head.

"As I will kill you," the man matter-of-factly agreed. "I would have preferred to finish the job at the hotel, but my employer is adamant on the subject of—a list of names? Information hidden by the professor for whom you worked—something you and Mr. Sterling now possess? Since my esteemed reputation depends on my ability to carry out specific requests. . . ."

He lifted Paige to a sitting position, and she moaned again. Her whole body burned as the claw-like hands tightened on her arms, administering a slight shake.

"You will tell me what I wish to know."

Through the pain and tears, Paige ground out hoarsely, "No! I won't tell you anything. . . ." Grief suddenly boiled up into an irrational anger as she stared into the slanting, opaque eyes. "You killed Jonah! I'll never tell you what you want. Never!"

"I can make you tell me." His hand gathered up her hair and twisted. "You are not used to pain, Miss Hawthorne. I do not think it will take me long to extract the information I desire."

Paige heard him as though from a distance and faced the humiliating reality that he was right. The pain he was inflicting now was making her lightheaded.

But from deep within she also knew she had been promised strength beyond her human frailty, and the grace to bear whatever portion was meted out to her—as she needed it. *Help me, Lord. I need you so much!*. Jonah couldn't help her now, but she couldn't think of that. She was going to fight—and then she would die with dignity.

She caught her lower lip between her teeth and willed her body to relax, pretending to cower. "All right. What do you want to know?"

"That's better." Abruptly, he let her go, and she sagged back against the cold concrete wall. The smug satisfaction in his voice almost goaded her into attacking immediately.

"I feel sick."

"Too bad," was the indifferent reply. "That will not prevent you from telling me what I want to know. . . . And I do not believe it will inconvenience you for long."

Suddenly he leaned over, his breath right in her face, suffocating her. The knife appeared in front of her eyes, mesmerizing her as it wove gently back and forth. The steel blade winked and glimmered in the flickering lantern light. "Who are these witnesses you mentioned? Where have you hidden the information Professor Kittridge discovered concerning my employer?"

"You mean Armand Gladstone?"

The back of his hand slashed across her cheek. "I will ask the questions. Each time I do not like the answers. . . you will feel. . . ."

The knife point pressed against the opposite side of her neck, drawing blood. Paige shrank back, in pain, not having to fake her mounting fear. She would have to make her move soon, or she would be too weak to do so.

"My purse," she gasped, praying the diversion would work. "I need. . .my purse." *Father in heaven, let it work . . .*

She felt him hesitate; the very air vibrated with suspicion. "I have checked the contents of your purse."

The knife rested against her throat. The point drew a drop of blood.

"I have to show you. . . ."

She waited, quivering, breath suspended. Abruptly, the knife lifted. "If you move, I will cut you where it will hurt— badly—but it will not be fatal."

Paige waited until he was all the way across the room. She took a deep breath, then lurched to her feet. *I will go down fighting, Jonah. You'd be proud. . . .*

"You little fool!" The man started back toward her. The

knife pointed at her throat.

"You can whistle for the information," Paige declared with all the bravado she could muster. There was nothing she could use as a weapon within reach; the battle would be short.

The sound of breaking glass caught both of them off guard. Even as the man whipped toward the sound, Paige dove behind the counter where the kerosene lamp sat. A rusted piece of pipe lay on the shelf under the counter. She grabbed it, rose, then froze in shock.

Jonah had flown through the window, landing amid the shattered glass in a graceful roll an Olympic gymnast would envy. He surged to his feet with lightning fluidity, in the same menacing stance Paige had seen him take months ago at Professor K's house.

He faced the astonished man in front of him with a savage grin Paige had never seen before. She knew instantly that she never wanted to see it again.

CHAPTER 23

Jonah stalked the assassin, moving warily around him, watching his every move, every flicker of the narrowed, calculating eyes, even the slight rise and fall of his chest as he breathed.

"Paige," he spoke without looking at her, his voice calm and level, "get out the door and take the van—the keys are in the ignition."

"No!" Her voice broke. "I won't leave you here—"

Suddenly, the man leaped—toward Paige. Jonah rushed him, catching the back of his knees in a low tackle that sent them both sprawling. Paige sprang back as both men jumped to their feet.

The duel was eerie, unreal as the two men fought in silence. The assassin had dropped his knife when Jonah tackled him, and it was lying on the floor in front of the counter. Jonah blocked a jab to his solar plexus and delivered a right jab to the assassin's cheekbone. The smaller-boned Oriental staggered back, then fell sideways as he grabbed for the knife. He grunted, then savagely kicked out. Jonah sidestepped, kicking the weapon out of reach.

The man sprang up, his arm pulled back. But as he jabbed at Jonah, Jonah grabbed his arm and twisted. The man dropped down, throwing them both off balance.

They fell against the counter, and Jonah's head crashed against the unyielding surface. His vision blurred, and he felt more than saw the hand chopping down toward his neck. He barely blocked the blow, but caught the assailant's foot and sent him flying halfway across the room.

He rolled as gracefully as Jonah; when he stood up, somehow the knife was in his hand, poised to throw.

Every muscle in Jonah's body tensed. Even as he ducked, rolling across the floor, he heard something hiss through the air from behind him—straight toward the assassin, who had to duck just as he threw the knife.

Jonah felt a breeze kiss his hair, and then the knife slammed into the wall behind him with a hollow thud. He jumped to his feet, but with the swift silence of a bat, the assassin darted through the door and disappeared, melting instantly into the night. Seconds later, the van engine revved, then roared down the road with squealing tires and racing motor.

Jonah stood very still, his breathing coming in labored gasps as his body throbbed in protest at the unaccustomed abuse. He turned his head, wincing at the pain, and watched Paige moving slowly around the counter toward him. She was colorless, except for trickles of blood from several cuts on her neck and great dark eyes the color of bruises.

"I thought you were dead," she said in the disbelieving voice of a small child. She came and stood in front of him, hands clenched tightly together. More blood oozed between her fingers from knife cuts on the backs of her hands.

Jonah took a shallow catch breath. "If you hadn't thrown that pipe. . .I would have been. And so would you." He lifted a shaking finger to brush away the single tear making a wet track down her face. "You saved both our lives."

"At the hotel—I heard a shot—I thought he'd killed you."

"It grazed me. I'm fine." Very slowly, he enfolded her in his arms, eased her against his chest, and began rocking her very

142

gently. "I'm okay, Paige. We're okay."

They stood for a few minutes, holding each other, absorbing the reality that they were both alive. Paige's hands couldn't seem to stay still, moving with poignant tentativeness up and down his back, so lightly she could barely feel the trembling touch. After awhile she lifted her head.

"Can we go to the police *now?*"

She was trying hard to smile, but it kept drooping, and the bruised gray eyes were suspiciously bright. Jonah cupped her face in his hands.

"The thought did cross my mind." His thumbs brushed the corners of her quivering mouth. "You'll have to ride the Harley again. . . ."

This time the smile stayed. "That's the best offer I've had all night."

For two days they pored over thousands of mug shots, but the assassin wasn't among them. A squad of technicians dusted the hotel room at the Castille and the filling station; the only legible fingerprints were Paige and Jonah's or hotel employees. There was no trace of the van.

"It's too bad he never took off the gloves," one of the detectives murmured late the second afternoon. "Obviously a professional. The *m.o.* sounds like he might be a west coast or European import. There's a guy we've heard about—did a couple of jobs for the mob. The only piece of ID we have is the fact that he's Chinese."

Jonah tested the waters by voicing his suspicion that a member of Congress could be behind the assault and kidnapping.

"It's possible," he was told by the cynical, world-weary detective. "In this town, anything's possible. But without some documented, reputable, ironclad proof. . .all you have is a lot of finger-pointing and nasty supposition." He grimaced.

143

"Which, when you're dealing with politicians, particularly of the congressional status, could mean a lot of rolling heads. One of them, unfortunately, would be mine."

He looked so disgusted Jonah had to smile. He stood, helped Paige up, and they turned to leave.

"Uh. . .Jonah?"

They paused at the door, Jonah's eyebrow lifting at the band of color that had appeared on the hard-bitten detective's cheekbones.

"I, uh, bought your last book—for my daughter. I was wondering. . .could you autograph it?"

The following afternoon Paige and Jonah were finally free to fly to Detroit and pay a visit to former P.O.W. Andrew McPhearson. They met at his house. A foreman at one of the auto plants, McPhearson was a short dynamo of a man with a glorious head of red hair liberally streaked with gray. He remembered Professor K and was shocked at his death. His opinion of Armand Gladstone echoed Slicks', though he chose his words more carefully.

"At first, I thought I must've been mistaken. Even in that bloody, awful war, it didn't occur to us that one of our own would deliberately set us up."

"What made you realize that's what he'd done?" Paige asked, taking notes even while the tape recorder documented every word.

McPhearson laid down the piece of wood he'd been whittling and gazed into the far distance. "They kept taunting us after we were captured, bragging on the guns and ammo we'd been sold out for. At first, I thought it was just a demoralizing gimmick." He smiled grimly. "They tried hard. . ." he stopped abruptly, shaking his head. "Anyway, about ten months after I'd been taken—they moved me to another compound, and there were some guys there who'd seen something really screwy at the infamous battle of Hill Number 418. They'd been undercover, watching for snipers, when all of a sudden, right underneath them comes this Army officer—and a couple of Viet Cong, talking as cozy as buddies in a beer joint."

Paige dropped her pen. "That's *unconscionable!* It's—it's treason!"

"Yes'm. I thought the same thing and swore that if I got out alive, some day that Army officer would pay."

"What happened?" Jonah asked into the little well of silence that fell.

McPhearson shrugged. "None of the others in my camp made it. I didn't know about the guy in Georgia. The war ended for everyone else—but the village where I'd been prisoner decided I was too useful as a slave. I didn't make it back to the States until '77. By then, all I wanted was to be left alone."

"Perfectly understandable," Jonah lifted the notebook from Paige's lifeless hands. "I read your story in the galleys of the professor's book. It isn't very pretty. I'm sorry we had to resurrect it."

"It was a long time ago. And with God's help, I've made a new life." He began whittling again, gnarled heads steady. "When Professor Kittridge started asking me pointed questions, and told me that that worm of a traitor was a Congressman, I couldn't just let the matter drop." He looked at them and said, very simply, "You need a character witness, I'll do what I can. The U.S.—not to mention the policymakers—gets a bum enough rap nowadays. We don't need any more garbage fouling the system."

Back in the car, Paige turned to Jonah. Determination etched each word. "Jonah, we've *got* to find some proof. It's not right. It's not fair."

"It rains on both the good and the evil, love. We just have to remember that God's perfect justice is at work even now, and somehow, some day—the man will pay."

"*They've gotten too close. They're stirring up too much interest. I don't care about the list anymore—just take care of them.*"

"*It will be done. I do not like failure. But my price is doubled. They will be extra careful now, and the police are suspicious.*"

The voice rose. "*That's your problem. Just do it quickly. I want them out of the way—now! If you can't do it by the press conference next week—I'll replace you, too.*"

"*Do not threaten me, Mr. . . . Smith. Or you might find that you have become the snake who bites its own tail.*"

CHAPTER 24

The day they returned from Detroit, Paige and Jonah holed up in yet another anonymous motel. Paige collated evidence and made a phone call to the Smithsonian while Jonah touched bases with various individuals who had been helping them trace names. He left, promising Paige he would be extra careful. Focusing all her attention on her work, she refused to dwell on the tissue thin margin of safety where she hovered—alone.

The previous night she'd awakened in a cold sweat, eyes staring blindly, seeing only a snake-like Oriental man slithering around her body which was blindfolded and tied to a stake. She hadn't mentioned the hit man or her dream, but its memory tortured her.

Jonah returned a little after two, looking windblown, cold, and disheveled from the first snowstorm of the season. The discreet patch of gauze covering his right temple was almost hidden by the tousled hair.

Relief flooded through Paige, and for the first time since he left, she felt herself relax. Jonah plopped down opposite her, slouching in the chair, with his arms folded behind his head.

Paige wasn't fooled. Excitement radiated from him, and the dark blue gaze fairly danced with secret knowledge. She laid her pencil down and stretched. "Okay—what did you find out?"

"How did you know?" He patted his pockets, eventually producing his glasses, which he absently crammed into place.

Paige snorted inelegantly. "What did you find?" she repeated.

Jonah leaned forward, tugging a folded piece of paper from his shirt. "Major Lamar Pettigrew was in Army Intelligence during World War II. When he died, he'd been in his third year of tracking down a number of Americans suspected of collaborating with the Nazis."

Surprised, Paige glanced down at the stupefying amount of material in front of her. It was all neatly arranged, in chronological order—but it all dealt with the Vietnam War. "I don't see," she began.

Jonah dropped the piece of paper in front of her. "The nine names," he reminded her. "Behind the ribbons bar? One of which was Gladstone?"

"I know all that. But all the evidence we've unearthed is about *Armand* Gladstone and what he purportedly did in Vietnam. He's much too young to have fought in World War II."

"Mm. Armand was—but what about his father?" Jonah leaned back again, closing his eyes. "Remember what the professor wrote on the piece of paper he hid?"

Paige slowly lifted her head. She'd read the words on that piece of paper so many times they were engraved forever in her brain. ". . .'Has to be the same family'," Her breath caught. "Jonah—it's his *father*!"

"Sounds like it. I talked with your friend, Major Haylee, persuaded him to let me take a dekko in some World War II files buried in the Pentagon basement."

"How did you—never mind." Major Haylee had never let

her beyond his office door. "When it comes to understated charm, the Lord truly filled *your* basket to the brim."

Jonah opened his eyes, bathing her in a warm study that caused Paige to duck her head. "We'll have to discuss its effects someday soon. In the meantime—"he tugged out another piece of paper and waved it in front of Paige's nose, "—I have here the last known address of one Everett Gladstone, attache for the American ambassador in England during the last three years of the war. Right smack in London he was—and right where our Major Pettigrew was snuffed. I thought a visit might prove informative."

"According to his son, Everett is very ill."

"I don't know," Jonah observed with a sardonic gleam, "that I can believe the word of the esteemed representative from Georgia."

"There is that. Where does his father live?"

"State of residence is—where else?—Georgia." He reached down and lazily lifted Paige to her feet. "And I'd be willing to donate my next royalty check to his retirement home if the old gentleman didn't enjoy a visit from Professor K last August."

"Is that where he lives? In a retirement home?"

Jonah removed his glasses, stuffed them back in his shirt pocket, and tapped the end of Paige's nose. "Nope. That's why I felt safe making that statement." He grinned cheekily, then told her, "According to some info I unearthed after my visit to the Pentagon, the possibly not-so-honorable Everett Gladstone resides in the town of Marshall, Georgia."

"How far is that from Warner Robins?"

"About thirty miles."

Paige began gathering up the papers and arranging them neatly back in her briefcase. Her fingers were not quite steady. "We're getting close, aren't we?"

"I think so. Um. . .Paige. . . ."

"Don't even think it. I'm coming with you." She looked up

at him. "I'm coming with you."

It was snowing in D.C., and raining freezing drizzle in Atlanta. The three hour drive south was tense with little conversation. The heavy traffic on I-75 moved at a crawl due to the weather.

At the Warner Robins exit, they joined several other cars of people who stopped to eat and freshen up at the roadside restaurant.

"I want to swing by the museum here on our way back to Washington," Jonah stated after the waitress left. "When I checked my answering service last night, they told me the curator had called. Someone's donated some more Luftwaffe stuff to the museum. I'd like to check it out."

"All right."

"Paige?" His hand reached across and covered hers. Paige lifted her gaze. "*Luz de la luna,*" he murmured, just loud enough for her to hear. "We'll be okay."

"What does that one mean?" Paige asked without much interest, too preoccupied to respond with her usual tartness.

Jonah's head tilted to one side, and he withdrew his hand to begin stroking his moustache. "It's Spanish, means moonlight. That's what you remind me of with your gray eyes and silver-blonde hair."

That did make her smile. "Yucch. That's really corny. Am I behaving that badly?"

"Mmph."

They finished eating and left after securing directions for Marshall, the small community some twenty-eight miles to the southwest where they would confront a hopefully off guard Everett Gladstone. The freezing rain had slowed to a cold drizzle. As he started the car, Jonah glanced over at Paige. "Corny or not," he drawled, "you *do* remind me of moonbeams."

Gray and brown, the gentle rolling countryside offered a dreary, depressing picture that did nothing to lighten their moods. Traffic was sparse, and the only one going their direction turned into the parking lot of a chain grocery store on the outskirts of Marshall.

They had no trouble locating Everett Gladstone. Twenty years earlier he had purchase a huge old antebellum plantation and had had it completely restored. According to the friendly convenience store clerk, the Gladstones were virtual hermits. She doubted if Paige and Jonah would be welcomed. The place was easy enough to find, however. . . .

Ten minutes later, Jonah and Paige were parked in a weed-infested circular gravel drive. They sat in the car a minute, staring at the two-story structure with four towering white columns proclaiming the glory of a long-dead era.

"Ionic," Paige offered, watching Jonah's gaze move over the house.

"What?"

"The columns. There are three basic types: doric, ionic, and corinthian. These are ionic." She opened her purse, pulling out a mirror and comb to touch up her appearance. "Don't tell me the widely-traveled J. Gregory, author of eight best sellers, never learned the basics of Greek architecture."

"If I kissed you in the car, do you think the person watching us through the curtains would be scandalized and refuse to admit us?"

Paige dropped her comb, watching helplessly in the little mirror as a blush washed up her cheeks. "It would depend," she mumbled back, "on if I let you."

Before Jonah could respond, she opened the car door and scooted out. Jonah followed suit, coming round and putting his hand under her elbow. He gave it a gentle squeeze.

"Whether lion-filled dungeon, fiery furnace—or the hundred-year old mansion of a family of traitors—God is walking

151

with us, love. What can man do, besides kill the body? Which, if you recall, has been tried without success several times now."

Paige squared her shoulders, but slanted Jonah an oblique look that made his mouth twitch beneath the moustache. "I'm okay with *being* dead—it's the process of getting to that point that scares the spit out of me."

Both of them laughed then, and the smiles were still in place when a pleasant-faced black woman dressed in starched pink opened the huge double front doors. In answer to their query, she informed them that Mr. Gladstone was resting in the library and could she ask their business.

"Tell him," Jonah said, "that we're here on behalf of Professor Emil Kittridge." His voice was bland, the deep midnight blue gaze transformed from teasing laughter to the hardness of polished onyx.

A minute later they were led down a hall and ushered into the library.

CHAPTER 25

Stooped and slump-shouldered, yellowish-white hair thin and dull, Everett Gladstone looked like a man life had chewed up and spit back out. He turned away from the floor-to-ceiling window, letting the sheer French lace panel drop back into place.

"I knew someone would come eventually." His voice was gravely resigned, the cultured accents slurred by age and infirmity. Moving with a slow, shuffling step, he made his painful way to an overstuffed chair and collapsed. Deep lines scored his face. Blue veins bulged in the bony, almost transparent hands.

Paige hurried to his side and poured him a glass of water from a plastic bottle sitting on a piecrust table beside the chair. To Jonah, the incongruity of that plastic bottle—which looked like standard hospital issue—struck with the force of a physical blow. He kept his face a mask and sat down on a loveseat across from Gladstone.

"Why did you know someone was coming?" he asked quietly after the older man had sipped some water.

For a brief instant, a look of cunning sharpened Gladstone's face, but it quickly dissipated, leaving him merely an old, defeated man. "Elsie told me you were here on behalf of that bull-headed professor. I tried to warn him. . . ." He shook his head, his voice trailing away.

"Warn who?" Paige asked. She shot Jonah a fierce look, but he ignored her.

Everett Gladstone's hand gestured irritably. "That professor—Kittridge." His gaze slid from Paige to Jonah. "Who else would I be talking about?"

"I'm not sure," Jonah picked up a porcelain figurine and pretended to examine it. "Perhaps your son. . .Armand?"

Everett seemed to shrink back into the chair. Beads of sweat popped out on his brow. "My son?" he repeated hoarsely. "What do you mean, my son? What has he done now—" He stopped, gasping.

Paige surveyed him in alarm. "Jonah. . .maybe we should call—"

"No!" Everett cut across her, the denial so forceful Paige stepped back. "Just. . .give me that bottle. It has pills. . . ." Paige obeyed, then sat by Jonah, hovering tensely on the edge of the cushion.

"At least Armand didn't lie about that, "Jonah mumbled half to himself. He leaned forward, dangling his hands between his knees in a non-threatening pose. "Mr. Gladstone, Mrs. Hawthorne was Professor Kittridge's research assistant for a book he was working on along with several other associates and scholars from across the country."

"Was?" Everett asked, his voice, his entire body vibrating with sudden tension.

Jonah ignored Paige's frantic signalling. "Yes," he answered, very gently. "Someone murdered him this past August. The police think he died of a heart attack—and Mrs. Hawthorne and I have been unable to prove otherwise, in spite of some clues we found. We've been investigating on our own." He paused, then added, "I have a feeling you might be able to help us, Mr. Gladstone."

"I'm an old man—and my wife's health is worse than mine.

What makes you think I could help you prove it was murder? He was a loud, obnoxious man, sticking his nose in other people's business."

"Would it help persuade you," Jonah continued smoothly, "if you knew that the professor's house has since been burned to the ground—deliberately? That both Mrs. Hawthorne's and my apartments have been vandalized? That there have been several attempts made on *our* lives—and the last one was very nearly successful?" He gestured to the scab on his forehead, then brushed his fingers over the band-aids still covering the cuts on Paige's neck. "We've been to the police—and even though their hands are still pretty much tied, we... um... have their ears, shall I say?"

When Jonah sat back, they could almost see Everett crumble, the shifting evasiveness of his posture giving way to bitter acceptance. "We need answers—proof—because the police can't help otherwise, and we can't dodge knives and bullets forever." He looked at Paige, knowing from the sudden sheen in her eyes that she was aware of how painful it had been for Jonah to be an interrogator—then a supplicant.

She leaned over and put her hand on Everett's bony arm. "Mr. Gladstone, we've been moving from motel to motel for several months now, running for our lives. I'm so tired—so frightened by it all. Tell us—please—about your son. About you—and what happened back in World War II that caused your name to be included on a list of names."

Gladstone buried his face in his hands. "How did you find out?" After a moment he lifted his head, staring at nothing but a painful past, a painful reality—and a probably painful future. With fingers that trembled, his hand reached to pick up the glass of water. So violent were the tremors that Paige put her hand over his to help him drink. He looked at her in disbelief—and shame.

"I'm an historian," she told him. "And I've been helping Mr.

155

Sterling with some World War II research in addition to the work I had been doing for the professor. "I found a piece of paper and a tiny key while I was cleaning and examining the uniform of an Army Intelligence officer. There were nine names on that list. Yours is the E. Gladstone, isn't it?"

"Yes." As if the stark confession had exhausted the last of his reserves, Everett leaned back, his head collapsing tiredly on the back of the chair. He closed his eyes. "So long ago. . .but it seems like yesterday. I never knew . . .no one ever came forward, so I thought. . .but I was always waiting. . . ."

His voice faded. Jonah and Paige sat quietly. Jonah glanced out the window, where the gray dreariness of the day was sliding into a sullen twilight without brightness, without the softness of the setting sun. He felt bone-tired, completely drained.

Everett began to talk in a low, dull monotone. "It was 1944. . . .The ambassador told me at a party one night that a man would be attending—a major from Army Intelligence. He'd been investigating some leaks, some damaging leaks, and had compiled a list of names of possible sources." He passed a still trembling hand over his eyes. "I, of course, was one of those sources."

"Why?" Paige asked, the word exploding out. Jonah wanted to take her in his arms and hold her, just hold her. She sounded so bewildered.

Everett shrugged. "It didn't seem so bad at first. I was young, and it was my first really important position. Geneva was so proud. I was approached, offered a lot of money, even more prestige. They said no one would ever know. All I had to do was phone a certain number, pass on pieces of information. At the time, the information seemed arbitrary, pointless, certainly not anything that would seriously damage the Allied cause."

Jonah ground his teeth, turning his gaze toward the shelves lined with volumes of books. He'd been all over the world, but the subtlety of Satan's snares never ceased to amaze and anger him.

"Then Geneva's brother died in battle." The old, empty voice faltered, then resumed the tale. "I found out that he'd probably been killed because of a piece of information I'd passed so easily over the phone. I told them I wouldn't do it anymore." He opened his eyes, looked across at Jonah, swallowing heavily.

"And, of course, they offered an alternative," Jonah stated without emphasis.

Everett nodded. "Exposure for me—slow, lingering death for Geneva. I didn't have any choice. I never realized. . . ."

"What happened to Major Pettigrew?" Paige asked.

Everett's mouth twisted. "I called my number and relayed the information that he was going to be at the party with the list of names. And I hung up the phone." His hands closed slowly into fists. "Making me directly responsible for at least one more death." He stared down at his clenched hands. " 'Will all great Neptune's ocean wash this blood clean from my hand?' Shakespeare had the way of it, didn't he?"

For awhile, the three of them sat in silence. Jonah studied the worn-out wreck of a man and mused over God's justice—and the ominous warning about the sins of the fathers. "What about your son?" he finally asked Everett slowly, reluctantly. "What about Armand Gladstone?"

The old man quivered as if Jonah had seared him with a branding iron. Wetting his lips, he thanked Paige when she held the glass to his lips. The look in his eyes was pathetic. "He found out what I'd done when I was ambassador to Thailand, in 1964. Armand was nineteen. He. . .never forgave me."

"What happened, Mr. Gladstone?" Paige queried, her voice soft, compassionate.

Everett looked down at her. "You're a nice girl. Why couldn't someone like you have come into my son's life before it was too late? My son, my son. . ." He cleared his throat, then swallowed more water. "My son stood there—looking at me as if I were Satan incarnate. He said. . .he said—" the throat muscles worked convulsively, and Everett's face had turned a mottled, sickly gray, "—he was going to continue in the family tradition. I—I asked him what he meant. He looked at me—through me. Then he said, 'You'll find out, Father. You'll find out.' "

Restless, feeling edgy, almost oppressed, Jonah rose and wandered about the room. It was a warm, attractive room with Aubusson rugs and oak flooring, waist high oak paneling and a heavy floral print wallpaper above. Silk floral arrangements completed the rose and forest green colors.

It should have been a peaceful, welcoming room, but it wasn't. Jonah moved and stood behind Paige's chair, resting his hands on her rigid shoulders.

"What did your son do?"

Everett looked at both of them, then out the window. "He joined the Army and secured a commission. For the first couple of years, he made a point of telling me—in graphic detail—of how he was selling guns, ammo, and military secrets to the Viet Cong. Of how he used the Gladstone name to rise in rank and power—and how easy it was. The one time I threatened to expose him, he laughed in my face—and said he hoped we wouldn't share the same cell at Leavenworth."

Jonah didn't realize how hard he was gripping Paige's shoulders until her hands lifted to cover his and gently stroke them, easing his fingers.

"That's the last time I saw him," Everett finished. He took a deep, quivering breath. "It's been twenty years now. . .I know he 'won' a seat in Congress—and I know he won it any way he could. My son has become an evil man, even though the public looks on him as a hero, a powerful man who is also—" his voice thickened, "—a true gentleman. And I sit here and

158

watch it happen—and do nothing."

The grandfather clock behind him struck four times. Everett rose. "My wife will be home soon. I don't want . . . ." The pleas faltered on his lips. He stared at them with old, hopeless eyes. "It never ends," he whispered. "The lies, the evasion. The fear. With me it was the prestige, the money; with my son, it started with revenge—but he's beyond that now. He's drunk on the power, as well as the money and position. And I can say nothing—do nothing. I did try to warn him after that professor came. I called him. He just laughed at me, secure that his congressional position would be more than enough cloak. It was hopeless. It's all a trap, a deadly snare that I couldn't escape—and now it's ruined my only son."

He gazed down at the floor, hands working convulsively at his sides. "If my wife finds out what you've told me—what I've told you—the shock will kill her." His voice trailed off. "It's been slowly killing me for almost fifty years, and now, my son. My son. . . ."

CHAPTER 26

The drive to Warner Robins was accompanied by heavy silence. Paige stared out the window and watched the eerie twilight fade into evening. The sky had cleared, and a full moon, barely visible right now, was slowly rising above the shell pink horizon in front of them. She watched the moon and thought about the dying, broken man sitting alone in his beautiful, dying mansion.

"I wonder if that car is going to follow us all the way to the museum," Jonah speculated out loud some minutes later.

Paige jumped at the unexpected sound of his voice, her thoughts jerking back to the present. "You don't suppose. . . ?"

Jonah lifted his foot from the gas pedal. "Get ready to duck," he murmured.

Paige glanced across at him. He looked about as concerned as the moon rising so serenely in front of them. She wove her fingers together and counted heartbeats while they waited.

The car caught up, flashed its lights—and passed, the glare of the lights momentarily blinding in the early evening as Paige tried to catch a glimpse of the driver. "Did you see him?" she asked.

"No—lights were too bright." Jonah shrugged. "I'll keep an eye on him." He brought the car's speed back up. "I don't think we were followed, but at this point . . . ."

Paige leaned back and closed her eyes. "I just wish it were all over."

"So do I, love. So do I."

The Robins Museum of Aviation was situated out the back gate of Robins Air Force Base. The museum closed at five, but the curator stayed late so Paige and Jonah could check over the Luftwaffe memorabilia. Paige fingered an old uniform almost indifferently; it was difficult to summon up much enthusiasm for Jonah's book right now.

Jonah, on the other hand, quickly became immersed in the task, his eyes behind the glasses intent, absorbed. Paige shook her head. Earthquakes, hurricanes, a world war, murder, and mayhem. . .Jonah the consummate writer would not be swayed from his goal.

She dutifully scratched out some notes on her pad and waited without comment while Jonah doggedly plowed through a bulging shoebox full of letters. At a little before seven, he finally gathered everything up, piled it neatly back into two heavy cardboard boxes and re-stuffed the shoebox.

"I think that will do it." He wiped his hands on his slacks, smiling at the curator. "Thanks—this was extremely kind of you—especially letting me have photocopies of some of the letters." The eager, hovering curator beamed at Jonah's British accent, not at all impatient with being kept beyond closing time.

Paige hid a smile. Jonah loved research as much as she did, but he hated having to accept the role of world-renowned aristocratic British author. His natural panache made him as versatile as a chameleon, though, Paige reflected. Her smile broadened as she watched him trying not to squirm beneath the onslaught of effusive praise for his books.

Diffident, absentminded writer, fanatical about his privacy.

161

Coolly capable adventurer who traveled all over the world with serene insouciance.

Compassionate friend whose faith shone like a lighthouse beacon, bathing everyone in its warmth.

Devastingly charming man who, over the past months, had somehow managed to slip past all her defenses, restoring her self-image in the process, making her whole again.

And she was in love with him.

Paige made an elaborate play of gathering up her notebook and the photocopied letters. Fear and insecurity at finally acknowledging her feelings played a tattoo against her heart. Did Jonah know? Was that the reason he was always so gentle with her? Her grip tightened on the notebook. Since David's death, she had kept her feelings in cold storage, hiding behind a professional mask not even Professor K had been entirely able to penetrate. But now—

"Paige? Got everything? Harry's ready to leave if we are."

Startled, she nodded, not meeting Jonah's eyes.

They exited through the back door, and, after another round of thank you's and promises to stay in touch, the curator finally said goodnight. He hurried down the sidewalk, disappearing around the corner of the building. Seconds later a car door slammed, an engine grumbled to life, then faded as the curator's car wound down the drive. Paige and Jonah lingered in the cool silence of the night, gazing out over the display of planes.

The moon had risen through wisping shreds of indigo clouds, a gigantic luminous pearl so close they could almost pluck it from the sky. It cast a serene mosaic of light and shadow over the fifty or so planes and equipment on display.

"It turned into a pretty night," Paige ventured. Even to her own hears the words sounded artificial and overly bright.

Jonah, hands stuffed in back pockets and eyes gazing

dreamily upward, murmured an inarticulate agreement. Paige bit her lip and sighed.

After awhile they began walking; when they turned the corner of the building, Paige shivered as a cold breeze blew through her hair and down the back of her neck beneath her blouse and bulky sweater. "It's turning colder," she observed, then stopped abruptly. "Did you hear that?"

"Hear what?" Jonah still sounded preoccupied, and Paige knew with a painful little lurch that he was still lost in his plot somewhere. Over the last nine months she had come to know the signs well.

"I'm not sure." She put a hand on Jonah's arm, forcing him to listen as well. The wind soughed through the trees, rustling and mysterious. But in the dimly lit parking lot, nothing moved except a lone piece of paper tumbling soundlessly across the driveway.

Paige finally shrugged. "It must be the wind and my nerves."

That finally penetrated. He patted her shoulder comfortingly. "You're just tired. We'll grab a spot of supper, and—"

The hand on her shoulder tightened; tension radiated from his suddenly rigid body. "What is it?" Paige asked, her voice ringing out in the deserted parking lot.

"A puncture," Jonah said slowly, warily.

Paige glanced across at the rental car, noting the slightly tilted rear end. "What a nuisance," she groaned.

Jonah didn't respond. The wind had died, leaving a poised, waiting silence. In the utter stillness, goose bumps raced over Paige's skin. "Jonah, what—?"

She didn't have time to complete the question. Jonah shoved her down behind some bushes close to the building, his body falling on top to shield her just as a sharp crack splintered the night.

Behind the granite slab of Jonah's body, she squirmed frantically, panic devouring her in savage, tearing bites. "Jonah!" Her hands scrambled at the cold wet earth in escalating terror. *She was blind, and he'd shot Jonah. Jonah was dead. Dead. . .and there was a knife at her throat. . .a hissing voice promising all manner of unspeakable horrors before she, too, would die. . . .*

Hard hands—warm, strong hands—closed over hers, stilling the frantic movement. But the voice whispering urgently in her ear was not threatening pain and death. Instead, it kept telling her she was all right—he was all right. They were okay, but she must be quiet.

The swirling blackness receded. Paige abruptly went limp, her breath shuddering out of her in a quivering sob of sound. "I'm sorry." Her head dropped onto their clasped hands. "For a minute, it was the hotel all over again." Though the choked explanation was delivered in a thready, barely audible whisper, Paige knew Jonah had heard when she felt his hands slide back up her arms, then release her. He kissed the back of her neck.

"It's okay." The words whispered into her ear like a sigh, soothing, calming. "But I need for you to stay absolutely still now. Promise me, Paige."

She tensed again, but before she could question him, another sharp *crack* splintered the night, bouncing in an echoing ricochet off the museum's walls. A scant twelve inches from Paige's nose, twigs from an evergreen bush splintered into fragments, and dirt exploded from the ground in front of their hiding place.

Jonah yanked Paige closer to him, his hands biting into her arms. They froze into absolute stillness, waiting.

"He's off to our left," Jonah finally whispered. "If we can get to the back, the building will be between us, and we might have enough of a start to make it to the base for help."

Paige managed a jerky nod.

"When I squeeze your hand, roll over and start crawling. Follow the bushes. When you get to the corner—run. I'll be right behind you."

Right behind—and shielding her with his body. "Jonah—" she swallowed, licked dry lips, "—don't do anything crazy. . . ."

He didn't reply, but seconds later, he squeezed her hand. Paige scrambled to her hands and knees, crouched as low as possible, and began crawling. Bits of bark and stone cut into her hands and knees, and the wet earth clung to her in clammy, sodden lumps. The pungent aroma of evergreen and humus stung her nostrils.

Suddenly, Jonah's hand closed over her ankle, jerking her flat. Paige lay motionless, not even breathing. When Jonah prodded her, she began crawling again, feeling Jonah at her heels, hearing the faint sound of his even breathing. At the corner she stopped, heart racing, and waited for Jonah's signal.

"Now!" he whispered urgently. As they leaped to their feet and ran, a bullet slammed through the metal siding of the museum with a harsh metallic ping.

"The planes!" Paige gasped out as she ran. "Hide in the planes!"

Displayed in long rows with narrow concrete pathways between, the assortment of airplanes sat motionless, looking in the moonlight like a grotesque collection of metal insects.

Paige ducked under the wing of a snub-nosed prop job, eyes darting, trying to decide where to run, where to hide. Jonah grabbed her arm. "Over here!"

Hand in hand, they ran like a pair of rabbits fleeing a pack of hounds. Two rows over, a half-dozen planes down, and Paige tripped, almost yanking Jonah down with her. He caught her upper arm, hauled her up, then yanked her under the wing of a cumbersome-looking C-47. Shadows closed over them, and they edged backward until they bumped into the slanting fuselage, characteristic of the tail-draggers.

Shivering, breathing in uneven gulps, Paige sagged against the cold, rain-wet metal and tried to control the shudders coursing in unrelenting waves through her body. Jonah's arm came round her shoulder, hugging her tightly.

When their breathing had quieted, and only Paige's leg jerked spasmodically, Jonah slowly crept back forward, under the wing, toward the nose of the plane. Ribbons of moonlight shimmered in streaming patterns, highlighting some of the planes in its day-bright white light, while casting the others in impenetrable shadows.

Paige followed even more slowly, her eyes restlessly searching. The shadows protected them—but they also concealed a professional killer who, at this very moment was doubtless slipping from plane to plane, just as they were.

CHAPTER 27

Across an open space free of planes, a shadow darted across a patch of moonlight, then disappeared.

"There!" Paige grabbed Jonah's arm. "Near the back of the lot—I think he's trying to cut us off, keep us from making it to the base."

Jonah turned, his arms coming around to hold her back close against his chest. Paige's voice caught, then steadied. "I only saw him a second—I think he went under those tall pines."

"Okay," Jonah whispered back. "Let's try to make it a little further down, before he has time to move in closer."

Paige turned in his arms, clutching his shoulders. "Why can't we go back the way we came now?"

"Because there's nothing beyond the museum but swamp—and the highway. He could pick us off without any trouble, not to mention any unsuspecting motorist who stopped to help." He cupped her face. "Paige," his voice was urgent, but the hands held her gently, caressingly, "—you've got to trust me. Promise me."

Unbelievingly, his voice faltered, and Paige felt as if she'd been suspended on a tightrope across a deep gorge—and the cable had just snapped. She gazed up at his face but saw only shadow—and the pinpoint glitter of his eyes. "I trust you,

Jonah," she promised, very softly. "I do trust you."

For a minute his head bowed, and she thought he closed his eyes. Then he kissed her swiftly, his hand slid to clasp hers, and they began cautiously edging toward the front of the plane. In the distance, Paige heard the undulating keen of sirens etch the night, and the kernel of despair she felt sprouted.

"Let's go." Jonah sprinted for the next plane, Paige on his heels. They paused for only a second before dashing across to a larger EC-123, the huge radome atop the fuselage distinguishing it from all the other planes.

Paige shivered, her breath escaping in icy tendrils of steam. She wrapped her arms around her waist while she flattened herself against the plane. Jonah motioned for her to stay put. Then—his body doubled in a stealthy crouch—he made his way around to the other side. Paige trained her eyes on the jumble of planes and equipment across the field, searching for any movement.

Where was he?

She heard Jonah returning but didn't turn her head. "Did you see anything?"

"No—nothing." He paused, then said roughly, "I'm going to try to draw his fire—I want you to run for that B-52 over there, near the road. The back gate of the base is just beyond, and maybe—"

"Forget it," Paige snapped, so upset she spoke louder than she should have. The words reverberated into the silence, as sharp as the crack of a rifle. They froze.

Crazy with fear for Jonah, Paige reached up and wrapped her hands behind his neck, then tugged until their faces were inches apart. "I won't let you do it!" she hissed into his ear. "We'll *both* try to make it to the B-52, or we play hide-and-seek until dawn. Together." Dimly she knew she was losing control, but she didn't care. Only Jonah mattered. "You big lug!" she choked, tears spilling down her icy cheeks in rivulets,

"I don't want you playing Superman anymore! I love you—mmph—"

Jonah's mouth stopped the flood of words. His hands bit into her shoulders, pressing her back against the plane as he briefly, thoroughly kissed her. "Hush," he murmured against her mouth, stifling the angry, half-gasping sobs. "Hush, now. I love you, too."

His lips left her mouth. She could feel him, incredibly, smiling. "You do pick your moments, don't you?" he whispered, dropping a last kiss on the tip of her nose.

"I won't let you do it," Paige repeated with mutinous determination, though her head was ringing from his casual declaration.

"Mm—then I guess we better—"

A bullet slammed into the hollow fuselage six inches from Paige's head. Jonah threw her to the ground. "Roll," he commanded harshly, his body following hers.

She rolled, over and over like leaves in the wind. When she bumped into the nosewheel of a plane, she wriggled onto her stomach. Another shot rang out and, beside her, Jonah jerked. Paige's heart leaped in a gigantic surge of fear. "Jonah!"

"The helicopter—over there. Body's close to the ground—better protection," Jonah ground out, the words riddled with pain. "Hurry, Paige. I'm right behind you."

Father, help us, please.

She ran, hurling herself behind the ugly, squatting 'copter in a diving roll that jarred the breath from her lungs. Seconds later, Jonah landed beside her. He lay unmoving, his body taut. Paige scrambled to her hands and knees. "Where?" she asked him, her hands searching, patting his chest and arms.

"Left side," Jonah managed. His hand came up to her cheek. "It's just a flesh wound—but I don't know how fast I can run . . . ." His hand dropped.

Paige yanked her sweater off, folded it into a pillow, then

manhandled Jonah's belt from around his waist. "Do you have a handkerchief? No—lie still. I'll get it." Her fingers slid under his back, frantically tugging even though she knew the movement had to hurt. She could see the dark stain spreading over his sweater, feel the sticky warmth as she carefully eased his shirt free. It was more than just a flesh wound.

The sirens she had barely registered earlier suddenly sounded closer. Paige's head snapped around. "Jonah!"

"I hear. . .pray, love."

"I haven't stopped." She choked back a sob when he flinched, and her fingers trembled as she fumbled with his belt.

With a throttled groan, Jonah managed to sit up, holding the handkerchief while Paige tightened the belt to keep it in place. Then she tied the sweater around him for warmth. He leaned back against the helicopter, his breathing harsh and ragged.

The wailing sirens stopped.

Into the abrupt pool of silence came the sound of a shoe scraping on stone, the crunch of gravel—then more silence.

With Paige's help, Jonah struggled to his feet. One arm clamped next to his injured side, the other wrapped around Paige's shoulders, he urged them deeper into the shadows. Paige glanced frantically around. The B-52 lay some fifty yards beyond, crouched like an ominous black and green lizard in its camouflage paint. To reach it, they would have to cross a wide swath of bare ground, bathed in moonlight.

"Paige?" The husky syllable brushed against her ear. "I want you to listen to me. . .we don't have much time. . . ."

Her throat muscles tightened in a spasm of foreboding. "Don't ask me, Jonah," she begged in a voice thick with anguish.

"I told you once that I needed for you to trust me enough so that if I held you over a sacrificial altar with a knife ready to plunge into your heart—you wouldn't struggle." With melting tenderness and fingers that trembled, he traced a path across her face to her chin, then down her throat. "Paige—love of my heart—the knife is poised. Do what I ask you—and if you can't trust me that much, then trust God to provide the lamb. Please—or we're both going to die."

"If I leave you here, you'll—you might—" She couldn't say the word. She closed her eyes, knowing she had no choice. Knowing the longer she hesitated, the closer the assassin crept toward them. And the less of a chance Jonah had of successfully creating a diversion. *Lord, I don't want him to die.*

She opened her eyes, lifted Jonah's hand and held it between hers. "What do you want me to do?" she asked.

For a timeless second he didn't speak, and Paige could feel the tension dropping from him like heavy, broken chains. Then he leaned down, inhaling sharply when the movement obviously caused pain. "When I give the signal," he breathed next to her ear, "run for that bomber. Once you make it to the other side—where you'll have a little protection and be in sight of the road—start screaming bloody murder." Even in the darkness, she sensed his dry smile as he added, "Literally. Hopefully the guard at the back gate will hear. If we're lucky, they've already heard the shots and are coming to investigate anyway."

He stopped. Paige waited, hands clenched over his in a death grip. "Stay in the cover of the B-52 until either the gate guard or the police can protect you," he finished.

"All right," Paige answered after a minute. "Jonah. . . what are you going to do?"

His hands turned in hers, lifting to press a kiss on the taut knuckles. "I'll tell you later. Paige?"

"Yes?" Her voice was strangled.

"I love you."

She lifted her chin, swallowing the tears. "I love you, too, but if you get yourself killed, Jonah Sterling—I might not ever forgive you."

"Guess you'd have to take it up with the Lord, then." He smiled, shifted; dropping her hand, he moved with painstaking caution toward the front of the chopper. Paige watched while he slowly crouched down, then just as slowly straightened. "Now!" he called out in a light breath of sound that barely made it to her ears.

Heart in her throat, Paige tore off across the field like a spooked doe. She didn't look back.

CHAPTER 28

Jonah threw a stone the moment Paige moved. From somewhere off to the right, closer than he would have liked, he heard the muffled thud of running footsteps.

Now all he had to do was prolong the game of hide-and-seek until Paige made it to safety. He pressed his side harder, wondering at all the television stars who acted like catching a bullet was about as debilitating as a bee sting. *Don't be Superman,* Paige had begged him, and Jonah grimaced. Needles of pain wove a barbed wire fence around his ribcage, making him light-headed and less than steady. He felt like anything *but* Superman.

He focused on a second rock clenched in his hand. It was jagged, rough-edged, and he was squeezing it so tightly it bit into his palm. The stinging sensation was preferable to the burning pain in his side. Breathing shallowly, grateful that at least the wound was on his left side instead of his right, Jonah lifted his arm. He threw the rock with all his remaining strength, aiming at a spot about ten yards beyond where he'd thrown the last one. The gunman wasn't stupid enough to fire, but maybe he was desperate enough now to accidentally reveal his whereabouts.

There. Darting behind the C-47 where he and Paige had hidden moments earlier. The gunman slid soundlessly into the shadows again, but not before Jonah had glimpsed the lethal barrel of his custom-made rifle and the infrared scope.

He began backing down the fuselage of the helicopter. Would his reflexes be fast enough to do what he had to do? The makeshift bandage had slowed the bleeding, and the pain was starting to subside into a dull, steady ache. He could ignore that for awhile.

And he had to until Paige could make it to the old bomber, then summon the courage to start yelling.

The minute she yelled, he'd have to make his move. He wouldn't have a second chance.

Her cry, when it rang out seconds later, shrieked as effectively as any siren. "Help!" she screamed, the sound racing back to Jonah with startling clarity. "Please, help us! Someone's trying to shoot us!"

Jonah's body shifted into overdrive. He barrelled out onto the concrete walkway, into the spotlight brightness of the moon. "For the Lord and for Gideon!" he shouted with maniacal irrelevance. "Over here, you bugger! Over here!" Then he sprinted back among the planes, dodging and weaving—and waiting for the lethal bullet.

In the background, never wavering, Paige continued to yell. Jonah dived in a flying leap behind some partially restored wreck of a plane. Paige's voice cut off mid-sentence.

No! Father, no!

Gasping, half-conscious from pain, Jonah struggled to his knees—to hear the sound of a stern voice talking through a bullhorn.

"This is the police. Throw down your weapon and come out with your hands up."

Spotlights clicked on, flooding the area from four different directions, including the area where Jonah was hiding. He decided it would be better to lie still a little longer. Vision blurred, he could just make out the flashing dome lights of a

174

police car through a strand of trees.

A different voice spoke from another bullhorn on the other side of the field. "This is Sgt. Wajeskowski of the Air Force Military Police. We have you covered. Please surrender your weapon and show yourself."

From among the planes on display came the crack of the assassin's rifle. A spotlight exploded, plunging a corner of the museum lot back into darkness. Seconds later, Jonah spotted the black-clad silhouette of a man running a broken path in and out of the planes, back toward the woods at the far end of the museum. Off to the left, an engine growled to life, and a military jeep roared into sight, cutting a diagonal path designed to intercept the fleeing man.

Jonah finally clambered to his feet, resting his head against the cool metal.

"Freeze!" commanded a voice behind him. Running feet approached.

"I'm the one being shot at," Jonah told the fuselage, and almost laughed. He was very careful to remain as still as possible, however, at the ominous clank of a round being chambered into an M-16. "Your bloke's headed toward the swamp."

"Sorry, sir—didn't want to take any chances." A radio crackled, and the MP spoke into it without taking his eyes off Jonah. "State your name, please."

"Jonah Sterling." He swayed.

The young military policeman stepped closer. "You okay? The lady said something about you being shot?"

As if mentioning Paige had conjured her presence, both men turned toward the sound of more footsteps dashing across the grass toward them. "Jonah!" Paige called out brokenly. "That's Jonah—don't—" She skidded to a halt beside both men, looking wild-eyed and incredibly rumpled.

In the harsh glare of the spotlights, Jonah could plainly see

175

caked mud, smeared grass stains, and several scratches running down her cheek. Her windblown hair flew about her face, and with a quick motion she actually stuffed it behind her ears. Jonah tried to smile.

Paige glared at the MP. "He needs a stretcher and an ambulance, I told you!"

"They're on the way, ma'am" the airman politely responded.

Gunfire erupted, a short-lived burst of sound. The radio crackled again, and this time the military policeman moved away to answer it.

Jonah lifted his good arm, but it was such an effort it was already falling when Paige slipped into his woefully weak embrace. She reached up and kissed the corner of his mouth, then gently pressed his shoulder, urging him to sit back down. He was too dizzy to resist.

Leaning his head back, he allowed Paige to cushion him against her shoulder. Something wet splashed onto his hand, and he managed to twist his head just enough so that he could look up into her face. "Don't cry. It's over."

"I'm not crying."

"I'll be okay, Paige. It's painful—but not fatal."

"Just be quiet and rest, do you hear?" He felt her hands smoothing through his hair, stroking his back. "I don't ever want to feel like this again." Her voice was shaking, but Jonah wasn't sure if it was from fear or the release of it. With great concentration, he lifted his hand and traced the contours of her ear.

"You put your hair behind your ear."

"I did?"

He almost laughed at her amazement, but even the thought made him wince. "You did. I love you quite beyond all reason, Paige Hawthorne—including your lovely ears." He could hear his words slurring and decided it would be just splendid if the stretcher arrived about now.

Paige's hand came up to cover his. She began kissing it, then holding it to her cheek, which was suspiciously damp. "I love you, *mayn heldish leyb.* . . ."

He could barely comprehend what sounded—incredibly—like a badly pronounced Yiddish phrase. "What?"

As he sank into the depths of a bottomless black sea, he thought he heard her murmuring next to his ear that she was getting a little of her own back, even if right now she did have him at a disadvantage.

The last thing he remembered was the touch of her lips dropping a soothing, feather-light kiss on the top of his head.

CHAPTER 29

Jonah spent the night at the Houston County Memorial Hospital, but the doctor released him in the morning.

"Bullet passed clean through," he promised Paige. "Didn't even nick a rib. Missed everything that matters. He lost a lot of blood, but not enough to worry me unduly." He patted Paige's shoulder. "Someone's looking out for that man, I'd reckon."

Paige looked beyond the doctor to Jonah, who was sitting on the hospital bed, buttoning his shirt. The doctor had examined the entry and exit wounds, applied fresh bandages over the stitches, and written out a prescription for antibiotics and pain.

"Yes. Someone is." Paige replied, her eyes meeting Jonah's and staying there. She felt an uprush of love so powerful she was afraid her feeling must show nakedly on her face. "You're *positive* he's okay?"

Jonah slid off the bed and took two steps to her side. He tucked the freshly washed strands of her hair behind her ears, eyes warm with approval when Paige's hands remained relaxed at her sides. "I've never been better," he said quietly. "Let's go home."

"I'm glad they didn't kill him," Paige commented some hours later. The flight attendant had just removed their dinner trays, and Paige turned so she could watch Jonah while they talked. "Probably no one but another Christian would understand—but as much as I hated what he was trying to do to us—I'm glad he's not dead. Did you find out how long he'll be in the hospital? They wouldn't tell me anything."

The navy eyes smiled into hers. "You must be slipping, then, love." His hand lifted to cup her chin and tug her closer, sharing a slow, loving kiss of ineffable sweetness.

It was delicious, Paige reflected muzzily, to kiss when you weren't running for your life. She smiled against Jonah's mouth, and he lifted his head, rubbing his nose to hers.

"About Syung Lee," he murmured, sitting back in the seat. He reached for Paige's hand and idly stroked the fingers while he talked. "One of the bullets penetrated his lung. He came through the surgery okay, I was told, but he'll probably be in the hospital a couple of weeks. Then he'll be remanded to the county jail. We'll doubtless be flying back down for his arraignment next year."

"It'll be awhile before the fat lady sings, won't it?" Paige sighed, and let her head rest against the shoulder on his uninjured side. "I want to visit Armand, Jonah."

He didn't respond beyond a momentary stiffening of his body. "Why, love? It's in the authorities' hands now. They have all the proof they need—or will when Joe Syung Lee talks."

"What if he doesn't?" Paige sat back up, suddenly restless. "All the information we gave the police is still circumstantial if Syung Lee refuses to talk. And Armand's father. What about him?"

"Ssh, love. Just be still—rest. Everything's going to be all right now." His hand stroked down her arm. "We have Someone watching over us, remember?"

"I know, but—"

Jonah sat up, winced, then carefully grasped Paige's elbows,

179

forcing her to look at him. His thumbs rotated a soothing circle on the insides of her arms. "Paige. Trust me. Trust the Lord. We're safe now. We don't have to hide; we don't have to scrounge the country for clues anymore. It's over. We can get on with the rest of our lives." He grinned a little. "Maybe finish the work on a couple of books."

"I still want to visit Armand," Paige insisted, her chin jutting stubbornly. "I want to confront him with everything we found out, just to see what he says." She took a deep breath. "Jonah. . . I need to do this, or it will never be over with in my mind."

"All right. All right, love. We'll go see Armand."

He was looking out a window when they entered his office in the Capitol Building the next afternoon. He curtly dismissed his aide without ever turning around. Hands clasped behind his back, tall and imposing, he continued to gaze silently out over the Commons. Sleet splattered against the glass, sliding down the panes in icy trails. Jonah quietly shut the door, then followed Paige over to a couple of maroon leather armchairs. They sat and waited as silently as Armand.

"You can't prove any of it," he eventually said. His voice was cold, confident. "I only agreed to this meeting to warn you not to try." He turned, facing them with glacial calm. "If you do, I'll slap you both with a lawsuit—and win. You can rest assured that I will win."

Paige held out the large manila envelope she'd been carrying. "You might want to have a look at this," she stated with a calm that was largely feigned, "since it includes all the information Professor Kittridge compiled. I believe you've been. . .um. . . *looking* for it?" She dropped the envelope on a table between her and Jonah, then carefully arranged her hands in her lap.

The arrogant self-assurance cracked a little. He took a step, his eyes shifting, narrowing. "Papers can be forged."

"—And witnesses bribed or eliminated," Jonah spoke up for the first time. "We've become painfully aware of your *modus operandi*. But I'm afraid, Congressman, that this time you've blotted your copybook beyond redemption."

Gladstone drew himself up even straighter. "That remains to be seen." He casually scooped up the manila envelope. "I plan to acquire a Senate seat in the next election—and *nothing* is going to stop me." With a contemptuous flick of his wrist, he opened the envelope and dumped the contents onto the table.

Paige watched, scarcely breathing, as he scanned the neatly typed pages she'd formulated the previous evening. He ignored the photocopies of original notes, newspaper articles, and a cassette tape.

After a few moments Gladstone tossed the papers down. "A loser and a factory worker—trying to smear my name after all these years? A crackpot professor well known for his eccentricities?" His mouth twitched into a crocodile's smile. "You're wasting my time."

"What about Joe Syung Lee?" Jonah was stroking his moustache, looking about as ruffled as a sleeping tomcat.

Paige, however, knew him. She stirred uneasily. "The police caught him last night," she told Gladstone, and gave him her own version of a crocodile's smile, "while he was trying to shoot us down at a museum in Warner Robins, Georgia. As you can see—once again he failed."

Gladstone's smile turned into a slashing straight line, and a tic appeared at the corner of his mouth. "I don't know who you're talking about."

"I rather imagine Mr. Lee will have no such difficulties pointing you out," Jonah drawled in his best bored-Oxford accent. "Something the matter, Congressman? You look, um, a trifle nervous?"

"Get out of here." His voice was flat, a sibilant hissing of sounds that raised the hair on the back of Paige's neck. He began stuffing everything back in the envelope. "I'll deny everything—they'll believe me. The two of you can prove nothing. Nothing!"

"We don't have to, anymore," Paige said. "The police have the original documents of everything we just gave you—plus Joe Lee. Professor Kittridge's death. . .burning his home—"

Gladstone turned on her with a fierce, ugly glare reeking of malevolence. "You'll regret this—" His hands half raised—and suddenly Jonah was in front of him. Paige realized she'd been pressing back against the chair and forced herself to relax her death grip on its arms. Compared to Armand Gladstone, Joe Syung Lee was a Sunday School teacher.

"It's over, Gladstone," Jonah pronounced with a gentleness far more ominous than the older man's threats. He took a step forward, forcing Armand to retreat. With casual fingers, he reached into his shirt pocket and withdrew the list of nine names, his gaze never leaving that of the sweating man in front of him.

"We neglected to include *this* list of names in your packet there. I believe it's something else you spent a great deal of energy trying to find." He held it out to Gladstone, who glared as if Jonah had offered him a cyanide pill. Jonah just as casually folded the list up and put it back in his pocket. "We talked to your father. He told us everything he knew—including his own treason —and your response when you discovered what he'd done."

"You can't prove any of it!" Gladstone repeated, suddenly almost shouting. "None of it!" He whirled and strode over to his desk, moving to stand behind it as if to preserve the illusion of his power and position. "In two days I'm holding a press conference to announce my bid for the Senate seat. You'll regret this interference—I'll *make* you regret it. I'll smear your names over all the tabloids. I can do it."

182

"Will you hire another Joe Syung Lee?" Paige asked, cutting across the vicious diatribe.

Gladstone dropped down into the desk chair, red suffusing his face, the tic at the corner of his mouth even more pronounced. "You'll be looking over your shoulders the rest of your lives," he spat. "I hope when they finally get you, it's slow and painful."

"That's enough," Jonah reached the desk in one stride and leaned over, planting his palms on the top so that his face was inches from Gladstone's. "You've nowhere to run. Your filthy life is about to be exposed, and you know it—especially when the press gets hold of the story. Public opinion makes a fickle mistress, Congressman—and maybe you *could* win it back. But even if you do, the truth won't change. . .your political future will forever be marred, tarnished."

He paused, then finished with implacable promise, "I'm a Christian, Armand, so I'm trying very hard not to be judgmental. But I can tell you this: the almighty God is not mocked. Every man on the face of this earth will face Him one day to answer for his actions."

The words hovered in the air, and Paige could tell the exact second when bitter reality finally sank in. She watched in disbelief while Gladstone crumbled in front of them.

"No. You can't do this. . .I won't let you. . . ."

Jonah straightened. "You've done it to yourself. You sowed the wind, Armand Gladstone—and now you're about to reap the whirlwind."

"Nobody will believe you." His hands moved spasmodically, opening and shutting. "I'm a United States Congressman, a war hero. . . ."

Paige stood and moved to Jonah's side. "You're a liar and a traitor, and it won't be long before the whole world knows it." She shook her head, feeling the last remnants of fear dissolving. *'And the truth shall make you free.'* You're so right, Lord. I

183

do feel free. Free—and whole.

She tucked her hand through Jonah's arm. "I think we've made our point, don't you?" She smiled radiantly at Jonah, then glanced over at Armand. "You know, if I were you, I'd cancel the press conference and come up with a plan to retire from public office—before you get kicked out."

She and Jonah started walking toward the door. Jonah opened it, and Paige turned for one last look. The honorable Armand Gladstone was still sitting behind his desk, stone-faced and silent. The manila envelope was crushed between his hands.

CHAPTER 30

"Y'know what we need to do now?" Jonah observed the following evening as he helped Paige clear the table in her apartment.

"What?" Paige turned the water on and began rinsing dishes. It had been pleasure beyond words to cook a real, homemade meal, to share with Jonah in companionable, *restful* silence. Even the spectre of David had disappeared. Jonah had refused to allow her to make dessert as well as the whole meal, so he had purchased a frozen cherry cheesecake. And Paige hadn't felt guilty at all.

"We don't have to go back to the police station," she ticked off the errands they'd been running the last twenty-four hours. "You called and verified that they'd sent someone to talk to Armand. We've settled the last motel bill and moved all our stuff back into our apartments. I finished proofing the galleys last night, and you—"

"I want to pay a visit to Justeen Gilroy. Share with her the, um—'rest of the story.' Within limits, of course." He placed some dishes in the sink and teasingly blew on the back of Paige's neck. "And—I want us to take the Harley. I checked the forecast tomorrow. Clear, sunny, highs in the fifties. A lovely, mild December day, perfect for taking a jaunt on my bike."

"I am not riding that machine all the way to North Carolina."

"It's only a couple of hundred miles. We'll be there in four or five hours."

"Fine. You take the motorcycle—I'll take a plane." She looked over her shoulder, grinning at him. "And I bet I beat you there."

"I'm sick of flying—aren't you?" He snagged her waist and whirled her around, completely off her feet. "Just think of the crisp wind, the fresh air, the freedom—"

"No."

"Hugging me close?"

"I can do that on the plane—not to mention any other time."

"*Mula sin corazon.*" He kissed her, then dumped her in the chair.

"Cut that out!" Paige laughed up at him. "A friend at the museum only told me how to say *heldish leyb*. I didn't have time for more."

"Ah, yes. I did wonder about that. Your accent was—and is—atrocious, *mi amore*." He stepped back, adroitly dodging her swinging arm. "Though it's flattering that you think I'm a brave lion, even if God has blessed *me* with a heartless mule."

"I'm definitely taking the plane!" She jumped up. "I'll call Justeen to make sure she's going to be home, then make a reservation." She turned around, tilted her head to one side and shot him a challenging look. "You leave when I leave for the airport—and we'll just see who gets there first!"

"You're on." He caught her close, hugged her. "Paige? You'll be all right alone now?"

"I'll be fine. Armand knows he's lost. There's a good chance he'll be taken into custody soon. . .and I just don't think he'll bother incriminating himself further by hiring another hit man. He knows that they know that we know—if you know what I mean."

They both laughed.

"It's going to be hard for me, though," Jonah confessed, sobering a little, "—letting you go alone."

She pressed her fingers against his lips. "I know. But it's like going to see Armand—it's something I need to do. Sort of the last hurdle back to being normal and self-respecting. The consummate Christian professional woman."

She started for the phone, then paused when Jonah said her name. Turning, her heart twisted in a peculiar spasm at the suddenly strained look on Jonah's face. Her smile faded. "Jonah? What is it?"

The deep blue eyes searched hers. He started to speak, closed his mouth, then took out his glasses and began whirling them. "I want. . .um. . .will you. . .dash it!" He tossed the glasses on the table, took two quick strides and grabbed her close again. "I want to marry you—will you have me?"

Before she could answer, he pressed her head against his chest, speaking rapidly, pleadingly over her head, "I know your first marriage was traumatic, full of mental and emotional abuse. But—God as my witness—I would never do that to you. I want to love you, protect you—cherish you. Help you become whatever God wants you to be. The Lord—not me." He began kissing her hair, her ears, her temple. "I love you more than I ever thought it was possible to love someone. I realize I have a lot of faults—"

Paige couldn't bear it. She lifted her head, laced her arms around his neck, and stopped the flow of pleading words with her lips. "I want to marry you," she whispered. "Because this time I'm ready to be a *good* Christian wife—not a perfect one. I've learned the lesson you've taught me." Emotion swelled, squeezing her heart, her throat. "You helped me see that even Christians can fall into traps—especially when we're blinded into trying to do things man's way, by his standards instead of God's."

187

Jonah held her a little ways from him, studying her. "So you're convinced you don't have to live by my standards?"

"Well. . ." she traced teasing patterns on the soft cashmere of his royal blue sweater, "I don't know that there's much wrong with your standards. . .but no, I plan to live by the Book this time. Not the gospel according to Jonah Sterling—or J. Gregory, for that matter."

"Does that mean 'yes,' then?"

"Only if you promise I don't have to sing in the church choir, join every committee, darn your socks—"

This time his mouth stopped hers.

Paige's flight was delayed, and Jonah met her at the airport, looking as bland and smug as a cat who had just finished a bowlful of cream. He escorted her out to the Harley without gloating too horribly, however, and by the time they were halfway to Justeen's, Paige was almost ready to admit he'd been right. Almost, but not quite.

Justeen met them at the door, the fragrance of fresh baked oatmeal cookies and hot spiced cider filling the air. A television blared in the background.

"Come in, come in. I've been about to bust a gullet waiting to hear the story. You say that list of names you found was a list of traitors, and my father had been trying to expose them when he was killed?"

They shared a judiciously edited story with her, having decided it would serve no purpose to expose the tragedy of Everett Gladstone and his son. It was enough for Justeen to know the circumstances surrounding her father's death, and that the legacy of the list had, at last, been an instrument of justice. Paige had turned the names over to Major Haylee at the Pentagon who would distribute them among the appropriate authorities, who could then make any decisions regarding further pursuit of justice.

A haunting memory of Everett Gladstone flitted briefly through Paige's mind; she had a feeling he, at least, had already paid a heavy enough price.

Suddenly Justeen slapped her hand to her face and rose. "Here we've been yakkety-yakking away, and I almost plumb forgot!" She scurried from the room and returned minutes later with a crushed, dilapidated cardboard box. "I found this last week, when I finally got around to finishing up cleaning the attic at Mama's. Remember, I told you I'd planned to do that, the last time you were here? I've been so busy, though, that I never got around to checking the contents. Some woman in England sent it to Mama about five years after the war—see, that's her name there on the box." She poured Jonah some more hot cider, then sat down, propping her feet on an empty chair and sighing with pleasure. "Anyway, I remember when it came—I was so excited." She chuckled reminiscently. "'Spect I thought it was a present or something. Then Mama never opened it—said it was some of Daddy's stuff. Apparently the woman's husband and my father had been friends, and Lord What's-it kept a few personal belongings of Daddy's. I guess he died a year or so after Daddy was killed, and his widow eventually gathered up this stuff and sent it to Mama—and she stuck it up in the attic without even looking. I was plumb mad. . . ."

While Justeen talked, Jonah had opened the box. Carefully, he pulled out a packet of faded, crumbling letters, an antique, pearl-handled derringer, a pen-knife—and a diary. He picked it up, looking across at Paige.

She stared a minute, then with numb fingers groped for her purse. While Justeen watched with unabashed curiosity, Paige removed the contents of her purse, then felt inside, her fingers hooking under the lining. With an indistinct scraping noise, the velcro parted. Paige felt for, then tugged out the crumpled envelope.

189

With not quite steady hands, she opened it and took out the dainty key, handing it to Jonah. He inserted it in the lock and twisted. The clasp grated, resisting—then released.

Jonah put on his glasses, and began to flip slowly through the pages. Paige rose and stood beside him—and barely suppressed an incredulous gasp when the names leaped off the page.

Sometimes in neat print, in other places a hurried scrawl—but each one legible—Major Pettigrew had written down all the details of the sordid betrayal of their country by nine individuals. Gerald Minton. . .Brewster Covington. . .Everett Gladstone. . . .

If Justeen had found that box earlier, and they had had this diary—

"How interesting—a diary," Justeen munched a cookie and watched Paige and Jonah. "I don't know if you can use it in your book. . ." her voice trailed away as she absorbed the disbelief, then rueful humor on the faces of her guests.

Jonah slowly closed the diary and looked up at Paige. She just looked back. Gently laying the diary back in the box, along with the other items, he gave it back to Justeen. "It was thoughtful of you," he said, "but I really think I have about all the information I need. . . ."

He rose, and they began moving out of the dining room toward the front door. As they passed through the parlor, Paige's ear caught the television announcer's voice. She clutched Jonah's arm and stopped dead.

"—Late last night. Cause at this time is unknown. To repeat: Armand Gladstone, House Representative from Georgia, was found dead in the study of his home in Georgetown late last night. Local authorities are investigating, but have offered no explanations at this time. Stay tuned to this channel for a complete update on the six o'clock report."

"Lands!" Justeen shook her head. "What's this world coming to, I want to know. So much violence and right in the

190

nation's capital." She glanced from Jonah to Paige. "I notice they were real careful not to say whether it was murder or suicide. Sometimes I wonder about those politicians. . . ." She held the door open. "Well, I just hope he had his affairs in order and was ready to meet His maker."

Paige opened her mouth, then closed it. A paradoxical blend of heavy sadness and heart-lifting release coursed through her body. She felt Jonah's hand close around hers, the warmth permeating, filling her up. She looked up at him and smiled.

Justeen watched the couple walk down the sidewalk toward their monstrous chrome and black motorcycle. She shook her head again, wondering why such an attractive couple would ride one of *those* things. Ah, well, they were young. An indulgent smile blossomed when she saw Jonah catch Paige up in his arms. They embraced, exchanged a kiss. Then Jonah swept Paige off her feet and tossed her onto the back of the motorcycle. He was grinning like all the heroes of the old cowboy movies Justeen loved to watch.

Paige was laughing, and it transformed her too-pale complexion into a lovely, translucent glow. She shoved playfully at Jonah, then strapped on a helmet. Then she wrapped her arms around Jonah's waist and hugged him.

They did make a nice couple, even if they were riding a motorcycle.

Justeen steeled herself for the deafening roar, and her mouth dropped in astonishment when Jonah kicked the starter—and they vanished down the street at a quiet putt-putt. Justeen went back inside and shut the door. "All he needs," she muttered to herself, "is a mask and a white horse."

She could almost hear the *William Tell Overture* playing in the background.

AUTHOR'S NOTE:
JONAH'S TERMS OF ENDEARMENT TO PAIGE

koneko	kitten	Japanese
hana	flower	Japanese
hatzvi	deer	Hebrew
Blume	flower	German
Schildkrote	turtle	German
min vacker radjur	my pretty deer	Swedish
chate	cat	French
luz de la luna	moonlight	Spanish
mula sin corazon	heartless mule	Spanish
heldish leyb	brave lion	Yiddish
mi amore	my love	Italian

If you enjoyed this book and want to write the author, she would like to hear from you. Write to:

Sara Mitchell
c/o Accent Books
P.O. Box 15337
Denver, CO 80215